For as long as Charis Lindfield could remember, she had been spoiled and pampered by her handsome father. Despite the awful rumors that raged through the household of his unsavory gambling habits and questionable business dealings, she could only think well of him. She no longer remembered the long months he spent away at London and Paris, but thought only of the wonderful moments when he returned — laden with silks, velvets and intoxicating perfumes—and swept her into his arms and kissed her fondly.

When Charis was barely fourteen years old, he died, leaving her penniless and suddenly, life would never seem the same again. Charis was reluctantly taken in by her aging Aunt Lavender, the sister of her dead mother. With Aunt Lavender, Charis was made to earn her keep, as much as Ethel, the scullery maid, or her only friend in the house, Comfort. Before long, Charis was lighting fires, black leading grates, cleaning silver and brass and scrubbing endless stone floors. Worst of all was Aunt Lavender herself — shrewish, fault-finding, critical and cruel — who never missed the opportunity to taunt Charis about her father.

(continued on back flap)

Ring The Bell Softly

By the same author

The Haunting of Sara Lessingham

Margaret James

Ring The Bell Softly

ST. MARTIN'S PRESS,
NEW YORK

Library of Congress Cataloging in Publication Data

Ring the bell softly.

I. Title.
PZ4.B4734Rk   [PR6052.E533]   823'.9'14   78-4001
ISBN 0-312-68239-5

ONE

Fear is a strange thing. It does not always come in the way one envisages, and certainly I did not think to find so fierce and primitive an emotion in the dusty, respectable offices of Messrs. Spragge, Brown and Mutton of Gray's Inn.

It was the most prosaic of interviews, or so I first thought, and one which Mr. Henry Mutton clearly did not welcome. He had already informed me by letter of the legacy from an old friend of my late father's; precise in the details of the five thousand pounds and the house on the Romney Marshes, which was the extent of the estate of Silas Martineau. He had explained meticulously how the money would be transferred to me, and was making plans to sell the house, which, he said, I surely would not want to occupy. Thus, the last thing he expected was to find that I had travelled from Bristol to London to discuss the matter of my good fortune.

He looked at me disapprovingly over the top of steel-rimmed spectacles. "There was no need for you to come to London," he said finally. "No need at all. I offered to dispose of the house for you, and. . . ."

"I know, Mr. Mutton, and I am truly grateful." I did not mean to interrupt him so rudely, yet I did not want him to think me unappreciative. Besides, the idea of selling the property on the Marshes disturbed me. Silas Martineau had left it to me; perhaps because he had meant me to live there. "Forgive me if

5

I am taking up your time, but although you gave me a most admirable account of the contents of the Will, there are a few questions which I would like to ask. I thought it would be easier if I came to see you."

"Questions?"

He said it sharply, as if I had accused him of some malpractice. I could see the pale blue eyes flicker over me, as if he were seeing me properly for the first time. I felt my cheeks redden, wishing I had had a more fashionable gown and cloak for so important a visit, but Aunt Lavender had not believed in frills and furbelows, and considered the dark grey alpaca of dubious quality to be more than adequate for the penniless daughter of a ne'er-do-well.

For the moment the thought of my gay, handsome father made me forget both the legacy and Mr. Mutton's accusing stare. The vision of his face was as clear and real as if he was sitting on the other side of the desk, instead of lying in a lonely graveyard for the past seven years. I had loved him with a deep passion, which was taking a long time to fade, and, as is the way of human kind, I remembered only the good things about him. I would not let myself think of the long months when he was in London or Paris, and the old house on the Yorkshire Moors heard nothing but worried discussions of where the next shilling for food was coming from, or how the servants were to be paid.

I just recalled the rare and wonderful moments when he did come home, laden with silks, velvets and intoxicating perfumes, and had swept me into his arms, his eyes crinkling with amusement as he kissed me soundly.

Of course I knew what people said of him. It was impossible to ignore the unkind whispers of the maids and the gossiping of the villagers, and it was no surprise to me, therefore, when upon his accidental and shattering death, Aunt Lavender, my dead mother's sister, travelled from Bristol to confirm the harsh criticisms.

She was a small, neat woman, with hard eyes and a tight little mouth, and it was clear that she derived no small amount of enjoyment from her task. She had not minced her words as she spoke of my father as a womaniser, a drunkard, and a gambler, condemning as she had looked round the cheerless parlour, threadbare with neglect. The house would have to be sold to settle the debts and, since she had a duty to her dead sister, I would have to go and live with her.

"There is nothing else for it," she had said bleakly. "You have no money, no education to speak of, and are barely fourteen years old."

I had wanted to cry; to defend my poor father. Instead, I had stood mute as Aunt Lavender set out the terms of her reluctant aid. I would have to make myself useful in her house, she had said, for money did not grow on trees. One of her maids would have to go to provide the necessary income for my keep. It was to be no life of leisure, but at the time I had not realised just how inhuman loveless charity could be.

"Miss Lindfield?"

I started, conscious again of Mr. Mutton and his hostile gaze.

"I'm . . . I'm sorry. Please forgive me."

I pushed everything out of my mind except the matter in hand, concentrating upon him with all my might.

"You said that you wanted to ask some questions."

"Yes. Why did Mr. Martineau leave me the money and the house?" I had not meant to blurt it out so abruptly, but my embarrassment made me gauche. "I knew that he was a friend of my father's, but had he no relatives of his own?

7

No children?"

The pause seemed to me to be interminable, and Mr. Mutton's expression was guarded as he cleared his throat.

"He had one daughter, but they quarrelled a few months before his death. He cut her out of his Will."

"It seems unfair that she should lose what was really hers." I hesitated. "What happened to her?"

"She went abroad. She has not been heard of for over ten years. You realise that Mr. Martineau has been dead for that length of time? He specified that you were not to receive the legacy, or even be told of it, until you were twenty-one."

"Yes, I know. You explained that in your letter."

My lips thinned. If only Mr. Martineau had known what I would have been spared but for that last instruction, surely he would have relented. I dismissed the bitterness at once. It was over now, and there was nothing to be gained by dwelling in the past.

"And there was no one else?"

"No one." Mr. Mutton was firm. "Now, if you. . . ."

"What about his wife? I suppose she is dead too?"

This time I knew something was amiss. The solicitor's face had closed up, like a shop shuttered for the night.

"Yes."

But the terse monosyllable was unsatisfying, and I was determined to ask more, however unpalatable Mr. Mutton found it. Doubtless he intended to charge me for his services, and thus could at least lay to rest the doubt aroused in me.

"When did she die?"

"Some six months before her husband."

We sat and looked at each other in silence. It was an almost tangible thing, and I could feel renewed disquiet creep along my spine.

8

"How did she die?"

I do not know what made me ask that, for it was not my business, but the question leapt into my mouth before I could stop it. Henry Mutton's skin was pasty now, and I could see the beads of perspiration on his forehead, despite the chill of the November day. I knew he would have liked to evade the query, but he was cornered.

"She was murdered." The words seemed to stick to his tongue, but finally he got them out. "Their housekeeper, you know. Woman was hanged, of course. A very nasty business. Mr. Martineau never got over it. He was a different man after that, and doubtless that is why he quarrelled with his daughter."

"How awful." I was shaken, wishing that I had not been so inquisitive, yet somehow I could not stop there. "Did . . . that is . . . was Mrs. Martineau murdered at the house which has been left to me?"

"Yes, yes. It was at Barley Farm."

"Is it really a farm?" I knew that I sounded inane, but by this time I was as anxious as Mr. Mutton to be done with the fate of Mrs. Martineau. "I had thought it just a house."

"Yes it is. Many years ago it was a farm, and the name was never changed."

Mr. Mutton gave another cough and finally took control of the conversation once more.

"So you see, Miss Lindfield, why it would be impossible for you to live there. The house has been empty for years, and since the . . . well . . . the unpleasantness . . . it has had a bad reputation."

"Bad reputation?" I looked up quickly. "In what way?"

The heavy shoulders shrugged, trying to dismiss the subject casually.

9

"Oh, it is said to be haunted, but naturally that is nothing but superstitious rubbish. Nevertheless, it is not at all a suitable place for a young woman, gentley reared as you are."

I bit back a humourless laugh. Mr. Mutton had obviously never known Aunt Lavender and her ideas of how the daughter of an immoral spendthrift should be brought up.

"Nevertheless, I would like to think about it."

"Think about it?" Mr. Mutton said it blankly, as if I were bereft of my senses. "Miss Lindfield, there is nothing to think about. You cannot live at Barley Farm. It is not only because of the state of the property, and what happened there, but because the Romney Marshes are . . . well . . . they are. . . ."

"Not suitable for a respectably reared female?"

"It is no laughing matter," he said severely, but beneath the severity there was something else, harder to define. "The Marshes have a bad name too. In the old days, it was a smugglers' haven."

"But surely not now; not in 1865? Are you suggesting it still harbours such men?"

His eyes slid away from mine, as if to make sure that I could not read his thoughts.

"No, no. At least I doubt it. But it is a desolate place, with nothing for miles around but dykes and sheep and scattered farms. You would not like it."

There was another pause. Then I said slowly :

"I will let you know my decision in a few days."

After we had discussed one other matter I rose, forcing him to do the same.

I paused at the door, amazed at my own temerity. Three months ago I would not have dared to argue with Mr. Mutton's down-trodden clerk, never mind Mr. Mutton himself. Now it was different. I was free and an heiress, and the heady

10

sense of power made my smile a trifle malicious.

"I will write to you and tell you whether I shall go to live at Barley Farm, or whether you may sell it for me. Meanwhile, please take no further steps in the matter. Good-day, Mr. Mutton, and thank you for your time."

I passed him in the doorway, not looking at him as I made for the outer office. Yet I had not needed to look again to be sure of one quite extraordinary thing. For some inexplicable reason, which I could not begin to understand, Mr. Henry Mutton was a very frightened man.

My new-found confidence lasted until the next day when I reached the door of the trim house on the outskirts of Bristol.

I stood at the front door for a while, unable to muster the necessary courage to ring the bell. It was absurd, of course, for there was nothing in the house to hurt me now but memories, yet sometimes they can do more harm than physical abuse.

That first day seven years ago seemed like yesterday. Aunt Lavender had alighted majestically from her brougham, signalling me to follow her, nodding unsmilingly at Comfort Risby, her housekeeper, who had opened the door to us.

She had been as good as her word, my Aunt Lavender. I really did have to earn my keep, just as much as Ethel, the scullery maid, or Comfort, who had to cook, scrub, and polish, despite her important-sounding title. And I scrubbed too. From five-thirty every morning until nine each night, Comfort, Ethel and I were busy about that showpiece of a house.

We lit fires and blackleaded grates; cleaned silver and brass; tackled endless stone floors and passages with buckets of hot water; made our own polishes with beeswax and turpentine, for Aunt Lavender said shop-bought ones were far too expensive. There was always something to be done, very often twice-over, for my aunt was a perfectionist, and one speck of dust detected in a room would mean that the whole thing had to be done again.

At first I thought I would die. My body ached, not only with unaccustomed labour, but also through lack of food. Although we had fared far from well in Yorkshire, I always had sufficient nourishment, the best tit-bits reserved for the master's young daughter. Here, scraps were good enough for Aunt Lavender's servants and for me too.

Worst of all was Aunt Lavender herself. Fault-finding, shrewish, critical, and cruel of tongue, never letting me forget my situation; never missing the opportunity to taunt me about my father. I dared not rebel, for what course had I but to accept her chill bounty? Sometimes, as my roughened fingers adjusted the wick of an oil-lamp, I longed to throw it at her and watch her burn into ashes. Instead, I kept my head bent, trying to shut my ears to her spite.

If it had not been for Comfort, I do not think that I could have endured it. She was a tower of strength, and we had become friends from the start. Often, despite her own mountain of work, she would take on some of mine : I am certain, too, that she gave me some of her food, although she would never admit to it.

I had almost grown used to the misery, resigned to a life of slavery and Aunt Lavender, when one morning three months ago, Comfort rushed into the kitchen with the news that my aunt had collapsed. I had stood with my mouth open, for I thought her totally indestructible. Somehow I had managed to get to the sitting-room and had stared down at her waxen face and closed eyes. By the time the doctor arrived, she was dead. The heart attack had been sudden and lethal.

12

After that the solicitor came, a small nervous man, who announced the unbelievable news that my aunt had left the house to me, together with a thousand pounds. Whether she had finally relented of her own harshness, or whether she felt duty-bound to leave her worldly goods to her only living relative, I do not know, and at the time I did not care.

I had thought all our troubles were over, and that Comfort, Ethel and I could go on living in Bristol, cleaning the house only when it was necessary, eating whatever we fancied, rising at the wickedly late hour of seven o'clock.

But it had not been so easy. The shade of Aunt Lavender was still with us. She seemed to pervade every nook and cranny, and I still crept about, too scared to move even a chair from its original position in case she should miraculously appear and demand to know what I was doing. Comfort seemed more subdued too, and Ethel remained a self-effacing shadow as before. There wasn't a ghost, of course, and Comfort and I knew it. It simply was that we could not forget my aunt, or what we had endured in her house.

Finally I threw off my black thoughts and touched the bell. Comfort Risby greeted me with pleasure. She at least had put on several much-needed pounds in the last three months, and her dark print frock and starched apron were new and becoming. Since I had become mistress of the house, she insisted on giving a respectful bob whenever she saw me, although I had tried to stop her. It seemed to me absurd, after we had knelt side by side, hands red-raw, scrubbing the slate floor of the wash-house, but Comfort was very conventional.

She brought me tea in the sitting-room, although I would have preferred to share a mug with her in the kitchen by the shining black range, but that would have shocked her. Things were different now, and she stood with hands folded as I

13

sipped my tea and told her about my journey to London.

She listened quietly, not interrupting until I had finished. Then she said:

"Can't say I like the sound of this Mr. Mutton, but he's right about one thing. The Marshes are no place for you. You're too young and pretty to bury yourself in such a lonely spot."

I smiled. No one had called me pretty since my father had died, certainly not Aunt Lavender. She had insisted that my thick auburn hair be drawn tightly back in the most unbecoming way, often commenting that my eyes were too large for my face and that she had always regarded hazel as an ugly colour.

"They might be better than this." I winced as I glanced round the room. Somehow, we had not been able to stop polishing and cleaning, and everything gleamed and shone as if awaiting my aunt's eagle-eyed inspection. "It couldn't be worse, could it?"

Comfort knew what I meant, but she was still doubtful.

"Might be. I know something about the Marshes. Terrible lonely, they are, with shrieking birds sounding like lost souls, and nothing but water and sheep."

"That's what Mr. Mutton said." I pulled a face. "He also said that once there were smugglers there. I asked him if there were any now, but he seemed evasive. You don't think there are any, do you?"

"Smugglers?" Comfort was busy pouring another cup of tea, avoiding my eye, or so it seemed to me. "I don't know. Maybe there are, maybe there aren't, but in any event, I doubt that you'd like the place."

"Mr. Mutton said something else too." I had not mentioned the untimely death of Mrs. Martineau before, but now it seemed that I should do so, particularly if eventually we were to take up our residence at Barley Farm. "He said that Mrs.

14

Martineau was murdered by her housekeeper."

I expected shocked alarm from Comfort, but she merely nodded.

"Yes, I remember the case. Caused quite a stir at the time."

"You remember it?"

"Oh yes. It was in all the papers, you see."

"What happened?"

Comfort shifted uncomfortably from one foot to the other.

"Don't know that I can recall details exactly."

"But you must remember some of them." I was watching her face, paler than usual. "How was she . . . that is . . . how did the housekeeper. . . ."

"Poison."

"How terrible!" I shivered. The room seemed icy, for the fire in the grate was as small as in Aunt Lavender's day. We could not bring ourselves to waste coal, although I could well afford it now. "Did she confess?"

"No, she swore to the end that she was innocent, but there was too much proof."

"What sort of proof."

"They found the poison in her chest of drawers with other . . . well . . . with other things. Best to forget it, Miss Charis. No point in dwelling on such wickedness."

Part of me wanted to agree, but there was another part which felt a compulsion to ask more.

"You said the poison was found with other things. What other things?"

"Oh, it were nothing."

"Please tell me. I swear that you are making me more nervous with your hints than if you told me the blunt truth." I tried to laugh to ease the tension which had sprung up between us, but my lips felt stiff. "What else was found?"

15

Comfort looked at me broodingly.

"A poppet and a hare's foot."

I gazed at her uncomprehendingly.

"A what? What is a poppet?"

At first I thought she would not answer me, but then she said reluctantly:

"It's a small figure, made of wax or sometimes clay. This one was wax, and it had a hatpin stuck through the heart."

My hands trembled and I put the cup down hastily before I dropped it.

"Comfort! What are you saying?"

"Nothing that wasn't said at the time." Her lips were tight. "Everyone said Mrs. Copper was a witch."

"Mrs. Copper?"

"The housekeeper. They were sure she had been trying to do away with her mistress for some time by . . . by such means. In the end, though, it was poison she used."

"But she said she was innocent?"

"Until the morning she was hanged, or so the papers said. No one believed her, of course, except perhaps her son, but he were a child, and no one listened to him. As I recall, he didn't live at the Farm, but in one of the towns on the coast with his aunt."

"What happened to him? The son, I mean?"

"No notion. Stayed on with his aunt, I expect."

"But why did the housekeeper kill Mrs. Martineau? What was her motive?"

Comfort shrugged.

"Can't remember, really. I think there was something said about a missing necklace. Mistress thought the Copper woman had taken it, and there was a quarrel."

"But Mrs. Copper was not dismissed because of that?"

16

"No, seems not. She stayed on, but there was bad feeling between the two of them after that."

"You seem to know a lot about it." I looked at Comfort curiously. "You didn't know Mrs. Copper, did you?"

"Me? Of course not." Comfort denied it quickly and forced a laugh. "Bless you, Miss Charis, I told you. It was in all the papers. Made quite a splash, it did, what with the witchcraft and all."

"Yes, I see."

There was a brief silence. Comfort put four small knobs of coal on the fire, arranging them with care, brushing invisible specks of dust away with a brush.

"How dreadful if Mrs. Copper was telling the truth. Suppose she really was innocent?"

"How could she have been?" Comfort straightened up. "It must have been her. There was no one else, and don't forget they found the stuff in her room."

"Yes, I suppose so, yet...."

"Now, don't you be upsetting yourself about this." Comfort threw off the unpleasant shadows of our conversation and was severely practical again. "It were all over a long time ago, and there's no doubt that she did it. But that solicitor was right. That's no house for you to be living in."

"We can't be sure until we've seen it." I glanced round the room again. It seemed to be standing on tip-toe, waiting for me to shift the precise position of the cushion in my chair, or spill a few grains of sugar on the mahogany side-table. "It sounds interesting."

"And isolated too, I'll be bound. The villages on the Marshes are far apart, you know. Just a few houses, a farm and some cottages; then nothing for miles. No, Miss Charis, you're better off staying here."

She followed my gaze, well-aware of what I was thinking. "We'll get used to this in time, never fret. Now I must be off. I've the dinner to see to."

When she had gone I rose to my feet, moving about quietly in case I should disturb someone. I hesitated in front of the large glass-fronted bookcase, wondering if I dared take one of the leather-bound volumes down to read, but deciding against it. Once a week, Comfort and I had had to take every single book out and dust it carefully, but I had never been allowed to read one. There was no time for such idling in Aunt Lavender's ménage.

I stopped by the fire, recklessly heaping six more lumps of coal on the feeble flames, feeling wicked as I watched them burn.

Henry Mutton's tale of the murder had shaken me, but Comfort's recollections of the event were even more disturbing. I knew practically nothing about the matter of witches and witchcraft, for such works of the Devil were never allowed to cross Aunt Lavender's pure threshhold, yet there had been a maid in my father's house who had talked of such things. I was only nine at the time, and no one knew that I had been listening to her from my hiding place on the kitchen stairs.

I could not remember much of what she had said, but odd snatches of her words came back to me now. She had spoken of something called the evil-eye, and how one should always avoid hares, because one never knew what they really were. I hadn't understood what she meant, but that night I had had bad dreams, and when I next saw a hare on the Moors I had screamed aloud in terror.

Perhaps Mr. Mutton and Comfort were right. Barley Farm did not sound very encouraging, and even if one had the good sense to dismiss the idea of the unfortunate Mrs. Copper being

18

a witch, perhaps there really were a few smugglers left in the area, bringing their illicit kegs of brandy and bundles of silk from the nearby coast to an eager market in London.

I dined that night in solitary splendour in the frigid dining-room which overlooked a garden as neat and well-tended as the house itself. The soup was good, but sparingly served; the roast rather tough. I hardly noticed either though, because it was far better than anything I had had for a long time.

Naturally, I had not moved into the master bedroom, for that had been my aunt's. Comfort said it was not proper that I should continue to share an attic room with her, and so my humble belongings had been moved down to a spare room. It was scrupulously clean, of course, but the curtains were faded, the carpet thin. I had arranged my simple brush and comb on the painted dressing table, but the place still looked unlived-in, as if I had merely come to stay the night.

I hung my grey alpaca in the cupboard, next to my one other dress made of the cheapest black silk obtainable. For a moment hot exasperation flooded through me. How absurd it was! I was the possessor of two houses, and six thousand pounds, yet this was the extent of my wardrobe. Even Comfort was better off than I, for I had lost no time in purchasing her two full-skirted frocks with pin-tucks on the bodice, and a thick shawl to keep her warm.

To-morrow, I told myself firmly, I would go out and order a dozen gowns made of the richest velvets and satins I could find, but even as I slid between the icy cotton sheets, I knew that I would do no such thing. It would take more than one moment of rebellion to dispel seven years of unrelenting discipline.

I lay in the darkness thinking of my father, wondering what he would have done in my position, smiling wryly to myself.

If my father had had such riches, he would soon have spent them, and as for burying himself on the Romney Marshes . . . that he would never have done. He had liked plenty of people about him, noise, gaiety, and luxury. I sighed. That is why we had seen nothing of him on the Moors; they were as cut-off as the Marshes.

That night I slept badly. Perhaps it was the excitement of the journey from London, or maybe the high wind which was rattling at the windows. Then again, perhaps it was my talk with Comfort about poppets and hares' feet which made me restless.

Finally I dropped off, only to dream of Mrs. Copper. Although I had no idea what she looked like, I could see a face very clearly, recognising her instantly, as one does in dreams. She was trying to say something to me, but at first I could not hear the words. Then it seemed as if she were shouting, to make sure that I should not misunderstand her.

"They hanged me," she cried, and her face seemed to blur in the folds of the nightmare. "They hanged me, you know, but I was innocent. I swear to God that I was innocent."

TWO

A week later I was still no nearer to making up my mind about the future. I kept pushing the decision away, as if I were afraid of it, filling my empty hours with the mending of worn sheets and pillow slips.

How long I should have gone on in such a state of woolly uncertainty I do not know. Perhaps indefinitely, had it not been for the letter which Comfort Risby received.

She told me about it one Thursday morning, after we had discussed the menus for the day. Why we troubled with such a ritual I cannot think, for we both knew that luncheon would consist of critens and a small rice pudding, and dinner of a thin broth, with a cheap cut of meat to follow.

"I had a letter to-day, Miss Charis."

Comfort was creasing her apron very precisely, as if it gave her something to do with her hands. There was an unexpected note in her voice which I did not understand. Besides, Comfort, like me, had no relatives or friends that I had ever heard of.

"Oh?"

I left it to her to go on, but it was obviously difficult for her, and after a while I said lightly :

"Whom was it from, Comfort?"

"I don't know." She was subdued, as if she wished she had not mentioned the matter. "It wasn't signed."

21

"An anonymous letter?" I was startled, seeing the unhappiness in her. "Comfort! What did it say? It was not offensive, was it?"

"No, no, at least, not to me." She hurried on now, still not looking at me. "It was about Mrs. Copper."

"What!"

I felt a sharp spasm of fear, and almost reached out for the security of Comfort's hand. Just in time I remembered that I was now mistress of the house, and that it was my duty to protect and help those who worked for me. Gone were the days when I could afford the luxury of burying my head in Comfort's bosom, crying until I was exhausted.

"Comfort, sit down and tell me about it."

She wouldn't sit down, not even though I could see that she was trembling, but now she was prepared to tell me the rest.

"Well, it said she was innocent; Mrs. Copper, I mean. It seems that she had offended someone . . . or something . . . and that was the way she was punished. Hanged, for something she didn't do."

"Someone . . . or something?"

I swallowed hard, and Comfort nodded.

"That's what the letter said."

"May I see it?"

"I burnt it." She met my eyes at last. "I don't know why exactly, but as soon as I'd read it I put it into the fire. It seemed . . . evil somehow."

"But who could have written it?"

"I've no notion."

"Was it dated?"

"No, I noticed that particular. No date: just my name at the top of the page, and then a line or two, like I said."

I was shaken, but after that first tremor not really surprised.

22

It was as if my dream had been broken, and somehow I knew that to hear of Mrs. Copper again was inevitable.

"What shall I do, Miss Charis?"

I smiled and patted her hand.

"Nothing, at least not for the moment. The letter has gone, so we cannot shew it to anyone to see what they make of it. Come to think of it, we don't know anyone from whom we could seek such advice, do we?"

"No. It's queer though, isn't it? What it said, I mean. Almost as if someone had been listening to us talking the other day. I wish I'd never mentioned that woman's name."

"Come, you are being silly." I heard the quaver despite her efforts to conceal it. "That could not possibly have had anything to do with it. No one heard what we said. There was no one here."

"Maybe, but. . . ."

"Nothing at all," I repeated firmly and gave her hand another squeeze. "Do you know, I think that this has made up my mind for me, and not before time."

"Miss?"

She looked alarmed again, but all at once I was light-hearted, as if a great weight had been lifted from me.

"We are going to live at Barley Farm. I have had enough of this house and of Bristol too. I want to forget the past, and that we shall never do while we remain here. You shall go to the Marshes ahead of me and get our new home ready. Hire servants: we shall need at least three. And get in a good stock of provisions, for we are done with scimmerlads and chitterlings. In future, we shall live like kings, or at least queens."

"But, Miss Charis, the cost!"

I laughed aloud, uncaring if the spectre of Aunt Lavender were listening or not.

"Money is no problem now. Indeed, while you are making things ready, I shall go out and spend a great deal more. I have no intention of becoming the new mistress of Barley Farm in these rags."

"But what shall we do when we get there? I've told you how lonely it is."

"We shall live in solitary comfort," I returned cheerfully, "and there must be at least one or two neighbours we shall get to know. Also, I shall ask some questions."

"Questions? What about?"

"Mrs. Copper."

Comfort's face was colourless.

"Miss Charis, you can't! You'll get yourself into trouble if you pry into things which are none of your concern."

"That is a chance which I shall have to take." I was bold, never guessing at the time just what kind of trouble lay ahead of me. "I'm not afraid, and I am intrigued by your letter and what you have told me of the case. And after all, it is something to do with me, isn't it? I have inherited Mr. Martineau's house, and that is where it all happened."

"You'll learn nothing from the Marsh folk. You're a stranger, not one of them. They won't tell you anything."

"We shall see."

Comfort was not quite done.

"It was so long ago. Maybe no one will remember."

I sobered.

"You remembered, and so did the person who wrote that note to you."

Comfort said no more, shaking her head as she left the room.

I wasted no time in writing to Henry Mutton, ignoring his first reply which begged me to reconsider. A few days later I received the keys, and packed Comfort off with ample money and my final instructions.

"I shall travel down in January," I said briskly, pretending not to see her long face. "Have everything ready by then, and don't look for a frump alighting from the carriage, for you will find that you have the most elegant mistress on the Marshes. Good-bye, and don't worry. Ethel will take care of me."

I watched the dog-cart out of sight and then went back to the sitting-room. It was strangely empty, as if Aunt Lavender had faded away in the face of my brazen and unheard of behaviour.

I moved a few chairs and altered the position of some ornaments, just to shew my independence. Then I opened the glass bookcase and took down one of the volumes. I even piled more coal on the already glowing fire until the elaborate brass scuttle was half-empty. After that I sat down and planned what I would do on the following day.

The first thing would be a visit to Madame Leclaire, for she was the smartest dressmaker in Bristol. I would peep in the windows of the furrier in Market Square, where, in the past, out of the corner of my eye, I had seen the soft seduction of fur capes and wraps. I would buy perfume and scented soap, and some powder for my face. I considered the possibility of rouge, but that might be somewhat fast, particularly for Barley Farm. But there was always Rogets, the jewellers. When I had first come to Bristol I had had one small gold locket, which had been my mother's, but my aunt had soon taken that away from me, saying it was not suitable for me to wear such baubles. Now, I would buy a string of pearls, a brooch or two, and a ring; perhaps even a bracelet. I would purchase silver-backed brushes and comb with a mirror to match; lots of coloured suede gloves in place of my darned cotton ones; kid boots and stockings, and a handbag to go with every outfit.

There was so much that I needed, for I did not even have a decent petticoat to my name, and it was clear that the weeks ahead would be well-filled for me with shopping. It was an exciting and satisfying prospect, and I sighed in contentment as I leaned back in my chair and began to read.

The print was small and the fire was burning my cheeks. Much as I had wanted to read Aunt Lavender's books, the dry account of a missionary in the African Bush was not nearly so interesting as the thought of my string of pearls, and my eyelids began to flicker.

Soon I was dreaming. I knew it was a dream and that it was a bad one, and fought to wake up, but my limbs were locked, my mind chained like a prisoner in a cell.

I could see the same face that I had seen before. The mouth was working frantically, the eyes wild. I made another attempt to stir, but the face did not go.

"I said I was innocent, didn't I? No one believed me then, but now you know it's true."

I moaned, trying to escape. Then there was a loud noise which jerked me back to consciousness. The heavy book had fallen to the floor, and as I bent to pick it up I could see that my hand was shaking.

I put the book down on the table, fully roused at last, and impatient with myself for my drowsy fears. I had eaten too much lunch, and was paying for it; it was no more than that.

Yet it was very peculiar. Twice, I had had that vivid dream, and there had been Comfort's anonymous letter with the same message.

But if Mrs. Copper really had been innocent, who had killed Silas Martineau's wife?

I arrived in the village of Haydore on a frosty January morn-

26

ing. The carriage rattled over the rough road as if it were anxious to be done with the journey, and it was not hard to see why.

The warnings I had been given about the Marshes had been no flights of fancy. They were barren and unfriendly, with a peculiar emptiness about them, heightened by winter's muted colouring. From the window I could see the black waters of the dykes shivering in the wind, catching a glimpse here and there of waving elms, stark on the flat landscape. I saw the promised sheep too; not white and fleecy as I had expected, but dirty brown in their thick, curly coats.

We passed through hamlets with a few small cottages; a larger house or two screened by trees; noted a couple of watchers and their dogs tending their flocks. There were a lot of birds, flying low, but their cries were drowned by the grinding of our wheels, yet I knew that their voices would have been mournful could I have heard them.

There were fine, imposing churches to be seen now and then, rising out of grey pastures to break the skyline; farmhouses and their straggling out-buildings; clumps of thorn, ash, and dismal willow, but not much else.

Haydore itself was in the most isolated part of Romney Marsh. As I stepped down from the carriage I felt a moment of doubt. In the light of that dreary morning it was bleak and lost-looking. A few houses shrouded in mist, a barn or two, some shacks, and an idle cart. Perhaps I should have listened to Mr. Mutton and Comfort after all. In retrospect, even the house in Bristol seemed to be cheerful in the face of this solitude. Then I shook myself and paid the driver, who was obviously impatient to be on his way.

I only had time for a quick look at the unexpectedly large and jumbled facade of Barley Farm before Comfort was there to welcome me.

I caught her hand, vastly relieved to find another living soul in that wilderness, kissing her firmly on her flushed cheek in my delight at seeing her again.

She exclaimed at my appearance.

"Why, Miss Charis, you look real beautiful. Like a princess, I do declare."

It was my turn to blush. I had not purchased outrageously fashionable silks as I had once promised myself I would do. Instead, I had contented myself with well-cut gowns and cloaks of good material and glowing colours. The sable wrap made me feel rather wicked, the French perfume confirming my sins. Worse, I had found Mr. Rogets' discreet little shop quite irresistible, and I gave Comfort my new leather jewel-case with strict orders to take the greatest care of it.

At the front door I paused for a moment and looked back, caught by a feeling which I did not understand. The silence was oppressive. No one seemed to be moving about; even the birds were gone now. It was not fear that I felt; that was to come later. It was just a sensation that, despite Haydore's seeming tranquillity, there was something very strong and alive throbbing beneath its surface.

I wanted to ask Comfort if she felt it too, but by then she was urging me towards the sitting-room where a huge fire burned in the wide grate. Everything was perfect. Comfort and the staff whom she had engaged had removed the years of neglect as if they had never existed. The Martineau's furniture was old, but in exquisite taste, and rich mahogany shone in the light of oil-lamps, needed even at the early hour of noon.

I exclaimed at the comfort of the chairs, the polished wooden floors and newly-scrubbed rugs, the paintings in heavy gold frames, and delicate china housed in a glass-fronted cupboard of finest ebony.

"It is lovely," I said finally, and took off my gloves to warm my fingers by the blaze. "Comfort, you have done wonders. How did you manage to do so much in such a short time?"

Something flickered across Comfort's face which I did not like.

"Comfort?"

"Aye, it's not bad is it? Of course, we had to have new covers made for some of the chairs and couches. Got a man and his wife from Lydd to do those."

She stopped, as if she did not want to say more, but I knew there was more to be said.

"And the furniture?" I was stroking the patina of a small table by my side. "Who would ever think it had been moulder-ing here unused for ten years or more?"

That was it. I had found the key, for Comfort shivered im-perceptibly.

"Was it hard work?"

"Not really." She gave a nervous laugh. " 'Course, it was all covered up, but it weren't in that bad condition. In fact, it were for all the world as though. . . ."

"Yes?"

"You'll think I'm a fool."

"No, I won't. For all the world as though . . . what?"

"Someone had been looking after it."

Our eyes met for a moment; then she shrugged.

"I said it was foolish. The house was well-locked up, and who is there, after all, who would want to come in here and tend the dusting?"

"Quite." I said it absently, turning to the fire. "Was it the same all over the house?"

"Yes, 'cept for the attics. I haven't done them yet, but they can wait. No cellars here for us to worry about." Her thick brows met again. "Odd that. Most houses hereabouts have cellars."

"Well, I daresay we shall do well enough without one." I shook off the renewed disquiet, determined not to let Comfort's words spoil my first morning. "I'm longing to see the rest of the house. It's much bigger than I thought it would be."

And so it was. The old part of Barley Farm had been built in the fourteenth century; the second and larger half added in much later times. It was really two dwellings joined together; a veritable labyrinth of a place as I was soon to discover.

"Yes, it's big right enough. It'll take us all our time to keep it clean."

"I won't have you working too hard," I said swiftly. "You've done enough of that. We'll get more help."

"Lord bless you, Miss Charis." Comfort was laughing, whatever had worried her before quite forgotten. "We've already got a cook, two maids, and me, and I'm not one to sit with my hands folded, as well you know."

"Still, if it becomes too much for you...."

"It won't."

"What are they like? The cook and maids?"

Comfort grimaced.

"Not what I'd looked for, but it wasn't easy getting anyone to come and work here." She looked almost old for a moment as she glanced down to consider her hands. "Not everyone likes the idea of ... well ... you know."

"Yes, I see. I hadn't thought of that. What's wrong with our new staff?"

"Nothing really, I suppose. There's Ellen Bocking, the cook, and her daughter Emily. Don't say much, 'cept to one another. Then there's another village girl, Agnes Stoop. A sulky piece, she is. I had to go to Lydd to get the scullery maid, Louisa Cockie. Funny mite with a squint. The others don't like her, but they'll have to put up with her. As I said, there weren't many what wanted to live at Barley Farm."

"Why don't they like Louisa?"

Comfort sighed.

"Well, it's stupid, really, but they say she's got the evil-eye, on account of her squint, you see."

"Poor child." I said it almost mechanically, but the notion did not sit easily with me either. "And what else have you got to tell me? Have Mrs. Bocking and her daughter said anything about the Martineaus, or Mrs. Copper?"

"A bit, but I wish you wouldn't. . . ."

"Come on, Comfort." I laughed. "You know I'm longing to hear everything and you won't put me off by holding back information. What have they said?"

Comfort gave in, knowing she was beaten.

"Well, they all agree that it was Mrs. Copper what done it. No doubt in their minds on that score. Didn't have much to say about the old man's daughter, 'cept that she run off before he died and hasn't been heard of since. There was another thing." She was fiddling with the tie of her apron. "I don't think they meant to let it slip, but it seems that round about the time Mrs. Martineau died, a young man was found drowned in a dyke just outside the village."

My nerves gave another jump.

"You mean he was murdered too?"

"No, no." Comfort shook her head quickly. "Weren't no talk of that. Simply an accident. Probably lost his way in the dark, for he was a stranger."

"I see. Did you ask them about . . . well . . . about the other things which were found in Mrs. Copper's drawer? That

31

poppet you spoke of?"

"They wouldn't talk about that, not much, anyway. Hinted that there was something, but when I pressed them they shut up like clams. The Excise Officers were here last week."

I looked at Comfort quickly.

"Excise Officers, here? Why?"

"Suppose they check things once in a while."

"You mean they think there may still be some smuggling going on?"

"Maybe, or perhaps they have to visit the villages now and then, just to make sure."

"Have you asked Mrs. Bocking about the smuggling?"

"I mentioned it, but she cackled like a hen. Said that was all over years ago."

"Yet the officers came here." I was thoughtful. "What else?"

"Nothing more, Miss."

The silence stretched on for a moment or two, punctuated by the crackling of the logs.

"I always know when you're hiding something," I said softly. "I used to watch you fool Aunt Lavender, but you never fooled me. What else, Comfort?"

She was really unhappy now, her brown eyes troubled.

"I don't know that I ought to say. It's just a lot of silly stories anyway. Why fill your head with such things?"

"Because I ask you to." I was firm. "Come along, I shan't faint or have the vapours."

"I hopes not." She was not too certain, but she could see there was no way of getting out of it. "There's a tale about this house."

"I'm sure there is. Is it exciting?"

"Frightening, more like." She did not share my enthusiasm for the history of our new home. "Seems that it once belonged

32

to a family called Lovelace. It really were a farm then. The eldest daughter, Joan, was said to be a witch, and after all her family had died of Marsh fever, Joan stayed on here on her own. Place got run down, of course, for she didn't care nothing for housekeeping. People was afraid of her, yet they came to her for advice and help in certain things. Then one day she disappeared."

"Really?" I was intrigued, trying to keep quiet the flicker of something else in the pit of my stomach. "Did she never return?"

"No. A year or two later a man claiming to be her cousin came here. It was he who sold the house to Thomas Martineau. That was two hundred years ago. Funny things were found in the house, so it was said. There were sounds too, but the villagers wouldn't talk about it."

"No, I don't suppose they would. It is a fascinating tale, isn't it?"

"More than that," she replied roundly. "We ought never to have come here, as I said from the first. And that's not all."

"Oh?"

I held my breath, waiting for the final blow which Comfort was clearly about to strike.

"No, it's said by the Bockings and others that there is a witch in Haydore. No one knows who it is, or so they say, but there's one here right enough."

"I don't believe it." I was short, because I had to convince myself as well as Comfort. "They are trying to scare you with their talk. How can you be so absurd? There are no such things as witches."

She looked at me sombrely, and even the blaze at my right hand was not enough to stop me feeling cold again.

"Well, we'll see, won't we? Time will tell who's right. Now

come and have some luncheon, Miss Charis. You must be starved."

The low-ceilinged dining-room was as delightful as the sitting-room. I admired the new carpet which Comfort had purchased in Rye, gloating over the graceful table and carved chairs, and wealth of silver and crystal on the heavy linen cloth.

Emily Bocking served luncheon. She was a tall, thin girl of about my own age, with hair like straw pinned up under a starched cap with long streamers. She had very pale eyes and a curiously flattened nose, and it was obvious from the start that she did not like me. I saw her take in my rose-coloured merino gown and the garnets at my throat and felt a spurt of sympathy. I knew what it was like to want beautiful things to wear, and understood her unspoken envy.

She answered my greeting in a low voice, mumbling something which I could not catch. Then she went silently from the room, leaving me to my meal.

I felt a glutton as I spooned the creamy chicken soup, and feasted on roast pork, with Charlotte aux Pommes to follow. After I had finished my coffee I went to the kitchen to pay my duty call.

It was a vast place, with a range large enough to cook for a regiment, and a scrupulously clean stone floor. Comfort had bought new equipment, but the white-wood tables and chairs were old, like the long clock in one corner. I glanced at the dresser, bright with new cups and plates, approving the cosy chairs by the hearth.

Ellen Bocking was as fat as her daughter was thin, but there was no mistaking their relationship. Ellen's hair was grey, but she had the same colourless eyes and smudge of a nose. She dropped a reluctant half-curtsey and answered me briefly, her reserve as rigid as Emily's had been. Agnes Stoop was a pudding of a girl. Her florid face was set in disagreeable lines, and her acknowledgment was of the briefest.

When I saw Louisa Cockie turn from the sink, I could see at once what had made the others dub her the possessor of the evil-eye. One greenish eye was straight enough under sandy lashes; the other ran right into the inner corner as if it were trying to escape from something which it had seen.

I chided myself for my unkindness, and gave her an especially warm smile. She was a sallow child and very thin, her hands nervous on the dish-cloth.

As we walked back to the hall I said to Comfort:

"That girl, Louisa. Does she get enough to eat?"

"Same as the others."

"Are you certain?" I was remembering my own lean years in Bristol. "She looks hungry to me. Don't leave it to Mrs. Bocking. You make sure that she has enough."

I left Comfort to her tasks and began my tour of inspection. I wanted to do it alone, and to examine my new possession at leisure. I had seen most of the ground floor of the newer part of the house, but I peeped at the study, the library, and had a quick look at the ample store cupboards.

My first shock came when I mounted the stairs to the upper landing. There, straight ahead of me, was a portrait of my father. I was so taken aback that I had to grasp the banister rail to support myself before I could take the final steps and stand in front of it. For a long while I simply stared at it. It seemed to me that he was almost alive again, smiling at me with painted lips, eyes alight with the artist's skill. I was about to call to Comfort to ask why she had not told me about the painting, but then I stopped. Of course, Comfort had never seen my father, nor even a likeness of him.

35

I wondered why it was there, deciding in the end that my father must have been a closer friend of Silas Martineau's than I had realised; after all, Silas had left me his house. I also decided not to say anything to Comfort for the time being. For some reason, I wanted to keep my special secret to myself for a while.

On the first floor there were five bedrooms with more cupboards and presses, and above, the attics which could be reached by a stair at one end of a corridor. I decided to leave those for another day, and went downstairs again to investigate the older part of the house. This was reached through a passage, and, once there, the atmosphere seemed to change completely.

I told myself that the two parts were just the same, but it wasn't true. There was something different about them. The old part was a lower structure, containing a small study, a sewing-room, a parlour, and one unfurnished room. Above, there were three bedrooms, but that was not all. It seemed that here, there were endless secretive nooks and excrescences which hid cupboards and twisting stairways of no more than four or five steps, leading up to recesses and yet more cupboards.

I even found a powder-closet with some dusty old wigs in it, and a short distance away another tiny room stacked with clothes of a bygone age. I was surprised, wondering why they had been kept. Perhaps old Silas had hated to throw anything away, or maybe it had been Mrs. Martineau who had insisted on keeping them because of the beauty of the faded materials. I reached out and touched a brocaded coat, feeling it dry and brittle to my touch. There was a wide window shelf with tarnished powder bowls, combs, brushes, and a bottle which had obviously contained scent. I pulled at the stopper, turning it hard until it finally gave way.

It was a strong perfume, very distinctive and heavy, and I felt a quick distaste. It conjured up something in my mind, but what I did not know. I put the stopper back quickly and returned to the parlour. This must have been Mrs. Martineau's sanctum, for the furniture was dainty and delicate in its lines, the curtains pale chintz. There were water-colours instead of heavy oils, and an embroidery frame next to a spinet.

I opened the bureau by the fire-place, feeling like a brash intruder. Everything was in apple-pie order; each drawer and pigeon-hole filled with note-paper, letters, and neatly receipted bills.

Then I began to feel cold. The light was almost gone, and I was anxious to get back to a fire. It was very lonely there too, and I began to think about Comfort's tale of Joan, the witch, who had lived here so long ago.

I wondered where she had slept, and what she had done all day long in the empty, neglected house. It wasn't a cheering line of thought, and I tried to put her out of my mind, only to find that I was considering the remarkable fact that Comfort had found it so easy to restore the house to its former condition. As if someone had been caring for it.

I stood still in the doorway, hearing the wind rising. It moaned in the chimney like a sad voice calling to me.

I hurried back to the main part of the house, crouching in the low chair and restoring life to my fingers. All the oil-lamps were alight, and a few candles as well. They drove the shadows off, and the uneasy reflections with them. There must be some quite rational explanation. The furniture was probably in a good state when the old man had died; the covers must have been tucked firmly round it, protecting it from time and dust alike.

When the last of my doubts were gone, I rose and went into

37

the hall. Soon, Emily would be bringing the tea in, but I needed to wash my hands and tidy my hair before she arrived.

My bedroom was green and yellow, the colours of spring, and before long I forgot everything else as I opened the great wardrobe and surveyed my new clothes with possessive satisfaction. They looked rich and opulent hanging there, waiting for me to wear them one by one. I shut the door and gave a small giggle. Whenever should I have the chance in Haydore to wear the crimson silk evening gown, my one real extravagance?

In spite of that dampening thought, I was still happy as I began to make my way downstairs. I glanced up at the portrait of my father, smiling at him as if sharing my amusement with him.

It was then that I heard it. A sound somewhere between a creak and a scratch. It was a muffled noise, yet loud enough for me to be quite sure that I was not mistaken. I paused, halfway down the stairs, transfixed as I waited for it to start again. When I heard it the second time I rushed down the last few steps and almost collided with Emily in the hall.

She looked at me loweringly from under her lashes, and I was forced into a hurried explanation of my undignified behaviour.

"I heard something," I said, and was angry with myself for sounding breathless. "On the stairs. A kind of . . . well . . . creaking sound. Emily, I think we may have rats in the house."

She stepped aside to let me enter the sitting-room, putting the tray down carefully before she replied.

"No rats here, Miss," she said shortly. "Been over every inch of the place, we have, and not a sign of one, nor mice neither."

"But what else could it have been?"

38

I motioned her to put my cup down on the table beside me, for I was not sure that I could trust my hand to hold it.

"Don't know, I'm sure." She was disinterested, anxious to be gone. "But not rats, Miss."

I did not argue further, for I could see that there was no point. I would have a word with Comfort later on. But as Emily began to make for the door, I said idly:

"Emily. Miss Risby says there is a witch here in Haydore. That's not really true, is it?"

She turned to consider me with those pale, unwinking eyes, her full-skirted frock and starched apron making her look plumper than she was.

"Oh yes, that's true."

"But, Emily, it can't be. There aren't such things as witches."

I thought she was smiling, but it might have been the reflection of the fire, for she was some feet away from me.

"There be witches, and there's one here. Like we told Miss Risby, no one knows who it is; just that there be one."

I wanted to ask more, but the door was closing behind her, and at last I ventured to pick up my cup, sipping the scalding brew to steady me. Emily had seemed very certain. No rats at Barley Farm, but a witch in the village of Haydore.

But if there weren't any rats in the house, what had I heard on the stairs?

THREE

The next morning I went for a walk. I had had a good sleep, without dreams, dismissing my earlier alarms as the result of excitement and a tiring journey.

The notion of a young woman going walking on her own in Bristol would have been unthinkable. Here, in Haydore, conventions of that kind did not seem important. Even Comfort raised no protest as I wrapped up warmly and set out to explore my new surroundings. It was a brighter day than the previous one, and a weak sun was trying to force its way through the clouds.

I was too busy looking about me to worry about the cold, for I was eager not to miss anything. Haydore was a long, strung-out village. At one end of it was Barley Farm and at the other, so Comfort had informed me, was an even larger house called Mortdyke, the property of a certain Mr. Mallory. Mr. Mallory, who had not lived there for years, had returned to the Marshes three months before to recover, so rumour had it, from the effects of an unhappy love affair.

Between the two large houses were a few cottages, stretched out along what passed for the main street, with a winding lane which led off towards Belzett's Farm. Further on still there were some barns and an old shack, and then another scattering of shabby dwellings huddled together as if for protection.

To the left was the ruin of an old church. If there were any with a taste for a Sunday sermon, it meant a trip to the next hamlet, for there was no longer parson nor parsonage in Haydore, but simply the empty shell of what had once been a fine Norman edifice.

There were no shops either. Comfort had already explained to me that our milk, eggs, and bacon came from the farm; that one of the village women baked bread for everybody, and that other supplies came in once a week from Elmbrook, five miles away.

When I got to the far end of the rough path I could see the top of Mortdyke through the trees. It looked gaunt and unfriendly, and I was about to turn back when I saw a man walking towards me.

My first impression of Dion Mallory was that he was a harsh man, with an equally harsh face. It was only when I took a second and more careful look that I realised the sharply-angled cheekbones and jaw were also beautifully formed, and that even if his dark brows were bent somewhat forbiddingly, the grey eyes themselves were clear, bright and very penetrating.

His tall, spare frame had nothing of weakness in it, and he wore his expensive clothes with a considerable air. He seemed as out of place in Haydore as I must have done in my new russet wool and fur-trimmed wrap.

We considered each other for a moment without speaking. I thought his thin lips looked hard, and it appeared that his frown was immovable, but no doubt he was assessing me as I had assessed him, and with an equally critical gaze.

He had raised his hat at the moment of our meeting, but now he managed a brief "good-morning", as if it were the greatest of labours. I was determined not to be cast down by his obvious disapproval, and gave a polite smile, which he did not return.

41

"I am Charis Lindfield," I said finally, for it was clear that he had no intention of saying any more. "I have come to live at Barley Farm."

"So I understand." His voice was deep but without warmth. "You will find it a vast change from Bristol."

I was surprised, and his teeth shewed briefly.

"Oh yes, Miss Lindfield, this is a small place. It is impossible to keep secrets here."

I wondered what he would say if I asked him about the unidentified witch, a matter which appeared to me to be a very well-kept secret. But, of course, I did no such thing. Instead, I said quickly :

"No, I suppose not. And you are Mr. Mallory, and you live in a house called Mortdyke."

"Precisely. I told you : there is no privacy in Haydore. You have only been here for a day, and already you have discovered so much."

He sounded terse, as if my knowledge of his existence annoyed him.

"Were you thinking of calling upon me?" His voice was cooler than ever. "It seems that this might be so, since there is nothing else in the direction in which you are going."

I was irritated. It was not my fault that Comfort had told me where Dion Mallory lived, nor had I designed our meeting. His off-hand manner and near rudeness seemed to me to be wholly unnecessary, and now it was my turn to be tart.

"No, Mr. Mallory, I was not going to call upon you. I was simply taking a walk, and on the point of returning home."

"Then I will not delay you." He gave a slight bow, his tone bored. "No doubt we shall meet again. In such a place as this I fear it will be quite unavoidable."

"He really is a most objectionable man," I said hotly to

Comfort as I shed my wrap and stalked into the sitting-room. "One would think I had been trying to pester him, instead of minding my own affairs and taking a short walk. I hope I do not see much of him, for he is not a person I could like."

"Don't suppose you will." Comfort was reassuring. "He don't mix with people much. I doubt that he meant to be rude, Miss Charis. Probably upset because of his broken engagement."

"The girl was lucky, whoever she was." I sat down, my temper still ruffled. "What could be worse than living with a man like that?"

"Living with your Aunt Lavender, maybe?" suggested Comfort slyly.

I had to laugh, and then I felt better.

"Yes, you're right, and perhaps there is a good reason for his ill-humour. Let us forget him. I saw no one else whilst I was out. You were right, this is a desolate place."

"Like I told you." Comfort nodded. "Still, the men will be at work this time of day, and the women about their own tasks."

"Who lives in the house with the green door?"

"Ah, that's Mr. Rolfe's: Mr. Bel Rolfe."

"Bel? That's an unusual name."

"Short for Belmont, so they tell me. He's blind, but a right nice gentleman."

"Blind? How sad. Was it an accident?"

"No, born like it. Did you see that shack further on?"

"Yes, but surely no one lives there. It looked so neglected."

"Aye, so it is." Comfort was scathing. "A slut, that's what she is."

"She? Whom?"

"They call her Tana. Don't seem to have any other name.

43

There's something funny about her. Got a wild look, if you know what I mean."

"I shall look forward to meeting her," I said dryly. "She sounds more interesting than anyone else I've heard of so far. What about that large cottage with the barn attached to it?"

"Heron's Cottage? The Cobbs live there; Isaac and his wife, Annie. She's the one what bakes the bread. Ten children they've got, and another on the way more than likely."

"There is one empty cottage. Who lived there?"

"A Miss Prentiss. She were governess to Mr. Martineau's daughter. When the girl grew up, Dora Prentiss moved there." Comfort pursed her lips. "Mrs. Bocking says she left very sudden like, last September. Went up to London, they believe, with not so much as a word as to why she had packed her bags and gone."

My enquiries about my neighbours were interrupted by the arrival of Emily with the coffee. She hardly looked at me as she filled the cup from a silver pot, yet I could sense her disapproval. I was about to speak to her when a bell began to toll.

I started, as if someone had walked over my grave. The slow, soft peal of a church bell was the very last thing I had expected to hear, and I said sharply:

"What is that?"

It was Emily who answered, handing me my cup, her lips tucked in at the corners.

"That be church bell."

"Yes . . . yes . . . so I gather, but the church is a ruin."

"Bell's still there." Emily was laconic. " 'Tis rung every so often to frighten away evil spirits. Can't be too careful."

I wanted to ask who was ringing it and why so softly. If Emily was telling the truth, and the villagers really believed it would ward off evil, one would have expected a good Christian clamour, not a muffled whisper which made the flesh creep. But Emily had gone, and Comfort had followed her, and so I sipped my drink and put the matter out of my mind as best I could. Rats, a bell ringing in a deserted shell of a church, a scullery maid with the evil-eye, and the offensive Dion Mallory. Haydore really was a most remarkable village.

My faith in Haydore, and in human nature in general, was restored two days later when I received an invitation from Bel Rolfe to take tea with him.

I was glad to accept, for I wanted to meet more people, and I was already prepared to like Mr. Rolfe and to feel pity for him. I could have spared my sympathy, for he needed none of it.

He was about thirty years of age and very good-looking, with dark hair, clean-cut features, and sadly blank eyes. His smile was as warm as Mr. Mallory's brief grimace had been cold, and he greeted me with a pleasure which made me glow.

His house was small, but comfortably furnished. I liked the old red velvet armchairs drawn up close to the big fire, and the gleam of silver and porcelain on the overmantel. The room was not cluttered, yet it seemed lived-in and intimate, like a reflection of Bel himself.

"It is good of you to come." His voice was soft and low-pitched. "We do not get many newcomers in Haydore, and another face is welcome, even if I cannot see it."

He was laughing at his disability, expecting me to do the same.

"I have been told there are no secrets to be kept here, so no doubt you have been told just what I look like."

"Indeed I have." Bel was poking the fire most expertly.

45

"You're very beautiful, and your gowns have caused more comment than anything else in the last ten years."

"Oh!"

He turned his head quickly, hearing the doubt in me.

"What is it?"

I had not expected him to be so sensitive to the nuances of the human voice, but then I had never encountered a blind person before.

"Nothing, except that. . . ."

"Go on." He was soothing. "Don't be afraid to speak. Too many people are afraid to say what they are feeling."

"Well, it is not that important." I was embarrassed. "It simply is that I would not want you, or others here, to imagine that I had bought new clothes to . . . well . . . to. . . ."

"To shew off?" His smile enfolded me again. "I'm sure you didn't do it for that reason."

All at once I found myself telling him about Aunt Lavender and those dreadful years in Bristol, and the madness which had seized me once I realised I was truly free. He nodded understandingly.

"There, you see. It is quite easy to explain things when one has a mind for it. Ah, and here is our tea."

I looked up as a thin old woman came in and laid the tray on a table in front of Bel. She must have been nearly eighty, for her face was wrinkled like a walnut, her eyes a rheumy blue.

"This is Jonet." Bel's slender fingers were already feeling for the handle of the teapot. "She is a deaf mute, I fear, but a hard worker and very good to me." He gave another infectious laugh as he began to pour. "I'm afraid that Jonet and I don't make a whole person between us, but we manage to rub along somehow."

He was holding out the cup, filled to exactly the right amount. I hesitated as I took it, amazed that he had managed such a feat.

"Practice," he said, as if he were reading my thoughts. "Not so difficult, you know, if you have never had the gift of sight."

He would not let me be uncomfortable about his blindness, talking of it so freely and without rancour that I soon forgot all about it, as we turned to other topics.

"There are so many things I want to know about Haydore," I said after I had finished a delicious sponge cake of Jonet's making. "But no one will tell me anything."

Bel turned to me, the black eyes seeming to consider my face, although I knew that that was not possible.

"I will tell you, if I know the answers." He grinned. "What intrigues you about such a place as Haydore?"

"Comfort says she has been told there is a witch here, but no one knows who it is."

His grin widened.

"I've heard that too, of course, but it's no more than a tale, you know. All villages have to have something. We've got a witch."

"So it's not really true?"

"How could it be?" He was teasing me. "There are no witches."

"Nor smugglers? I believe the Excise men were here not long ago."

"Yes, they come from time to time, but only to satisfy themselves that all is well. We did have smugglers, of course. Famous for it at one time, but, alas, even that you cannot look forward to, Miss Lindfield. They've all gone now. I hope you're not too disappointed."

"No wonder you laugh at me." I did not mind his amuse-

47

ment, for it was so kind. "It does sound silly, doesn't it? And I heard a strange creaking noise a few nights ago at Barley Farm. I thought it was rats, but Emily insists there are none there."

"Emily Bocking? Ah yes, well she would, wouldn't she? She is very house-proud, like her mother. The thought of rats or mice would be an insult to her industry."

"Yes, of course, I see. And then there's the church bell."

"Oh, you heard it the other day, did you? Yes, that's a village custom. Wards off the Devil, they hope."

"Who rings it?"

He shrugged. "I have no idea. No one does. They just accept that it rings. More tea?"

We spent another contented half-hour talking of music. Then I said casually:

"Do you know Dion Mallory?"

Bel was looking towards the fire, and so I could not see the expression on his face, but when he spoke there was, for the first time, a slight restraint in his voice.

"We have met once or twice since he came back. He has been away for years, of course. Are you acquainted with him?"

"Not really. We encountered one another a day or two ago when I was out walking. I thought him very uncivil."

"Yes." Bel's tone was still reserved. "So I believe. A wealthy man, and a bad enemy; that's what they say of him." He turned, a faint smile back on his lips. "Perhaps he's more dangerous than the phantom witch, the rats, and the church bell all rolled into one. Be careful of him, Miss Lindfield, for he at least is real."

The next of my neighbours to cross my path was Henry Jones. He was an untidy young man of some twenty years or so, and he resided in one of the mean little cottages at the far end of the village.

When we saw each other, he pulled off his cap quickly, letting the wind ruffle his thick hair, the colour of pale corn. He flushed slightly as I nodded to him.

"I'm Charis Lindfield," I said, before his shyness could become confusion. "I live at Barley Farm. We ought to wait for a formal introduction, I suppose, but there seems no one about to do us that service."

He mumbled something, and held out a jerky hand to take mine.

"I'm Henry Jones, and I live down there." He pointed in the direction of the cottages. "I knew you'd come. There was talk."

"I'm sure there was. Everyone seems to know me already; I swear I feel quite famous." I was trying to put him at his ease, but I could tell that that would be no light task. "Have you lived here all your life?"

He shook his head, almost curtly, as if he resented the question.

"No. I've only been here a week or two. I'm writing a book, you see, about the wild birds of the Marshes."

"How fascinating." I was genuinely interested. "You like birds, Mr. Jones?"

He gave the question the disdainful silence it deserved, and I was forced to try again.

"Yes, of course you must. That was foolish of me. Do you live alone?"

Again I could see the withdrawal behind the light blue eyes, as if he was trying to shrink away from my impertinent interrogation.

"Yes . . . yes, I do."

"Alone, but not lonely, I hope?"

"No, no. No time to be lonely. Too much to do. I must go, Miss Lindfield." Henry had clearly had enough of me. "I expect we shall . . . shall . . . well. . . ."

"Yes, I expect we shall," I said resignedly, and watched him stride off. "In such a place as this, how can we possibly avoid it!"

A whole week went by before I met Tana. It was no accident that I was passing her shack, for since Comfort had mentioned her name I had been hoping to catch a glimpse of her.

It was a typical January day, very overcast, and I was beginning to regret my curiosity when I saw the shack door open, and in another moment Tana was there in front of me.

I am not sure what I had expected. Comfort had said she was a slut, and so I suppose I had formed a mental image of a girl with dirty hands and hair matted about a sullen face. I could not have been further from the truth in my muddled thoughts.

Tana was the most beautiful woman I had ever seen. Her long dark hair was black as night and gleamed with a sheen such as I had never seen before. Her sloe eyes tilted slightly at the corners, her nose was small and straight, her mouth as near perfection as one could wish. Far from being dirty, her white skin was spotlessly clean, and even though she wore an old gown and shawl, every movement of her body was like poetry.

I had the strangest feeling that I had seen her before somewhere; that there was something familiar about her face. Of course that was not possible. If I really had seen Tana before, I would have remembered her, for she was not a person readily forgotten.

She smiled at me, not with the easy kindness of Bel Rolfe, yet she was not unfriendly.

"Hello." Her voice was clear and reminded me of water running over stones, although why such a fanciful notion should come into my head I had no idea. "You're Charis, aren't you. I'm Tana."

She did not seem to bother with the formality of surnames, but that seemed entirely natural. She was not a formal woman. She moved her head, so that the long tresses were thrown over her shoulder, one slim hand brushing a strand from her brow.

"Do you like it here?"

"I . . . I . . . think so. I haven't been here long, but. . . ."

"I love it." She did not seem to have heard my answer, or if she had, she was not much concerned with it. "I have lived here all my life; there is nowhere else I would want to be."

Since Tana was dispensing with conventions, I did the same.

"Aren't you lonely? There is no one living with you, is there?"

The red lips parted briefly, as if I had made a joke.

"No, I am alone, but not lonely. How could one be here?"

I was spared the difficulty of finding a suitable answer, for Tana was moving nearer to me. The grace of her body was breathtaking, and I realised that for the first time in my life I was seeing a really sensuous woman. I stopped to consider what my father would have thought of her. He would have made love to her, of course, for she was the kind of creature he adored, or so Aunt Lavender would have had me believe.

"Have they told you the story of your house?" She did not seem aware of the elements, despite the biting wind which was chilling me, even in my heavy cloak. "Does it frighten you?"

"I . . . no, of course not."

"I expect it does really." There was no offence in her words;

51

she was simply being honest. "Don't worry. Perhaps nothing will happen to you."

"Happen to me?" I could feel myself grow pale. "What do you mean, happen to me? What could happen?"

Her slender shoulders rose negligently.

"Many things, pretty Charis, but then again perhaps nothing."

"You are thinking of Mrs. Martineau and what became of her?"

I don't know why I said it, but I wanted to see what the very truthful Tana's reaction would be. All I got was a faint movement of her lips.

"You knew her?" I decided to press the point. Tana should not have all her own way in this conversation. "If you have lived here all your life, you must have known her, and Mrs. Copper too."

The wind whipped at our skirts, shrieking over the Marshes. It seemed that Tana and I were in a small world of our own; as if there were no other people anywhere. Just she and I and the hostile marshes stretching off into infinity. I had a sudden urge to run, but then Tana said quietly :

"I knew them. Foolish Mrs. Copper. She shouldn't have done it."

"Killed her mistress, you mean?"

The dark eyes were examining my face, as if each line and curve were being imprinted on Tana's memory, but she did not answer.

It was exasperating. I was certain that Tana knew a good deal about Mrs. Copper, but it was going to be difficult to make her admit it if she chose to keep silent.

"Tana, I am not merely prying. I am living in Mrs. Martineau's house now, and it seems important to me to know what really occurred. No one will talk much about it. Tell me, please, did Mrs. Copper kill her?"

"She was hanged." Tana turned away from me to look over the Marshes. "Early one morning they did it. Foolish, foolish Mrs. Copper."

Even in my impatience I noticed that Tana said "foolish Mrs. Copper" and not "wicked Mrs. Copper", as one might expect.

"Yes, but did she... ?"

"Who else?" Tana glanced back at me, a suspicion of mirth round the corners of her mouth. "Take care of yourself, pretty Charis."

She moved towards the shack, and I said hastily :

"Tana, wait !"

She paused unhurriedly, turning to look at me over her shoulder.

"Yes?"

"Did you ... that is. ... Well, it sounds a foolish question, I know, but did you write to Comfort Risby at Bristol?"

The expression on her face did not change, and I saw a gust lift her hair until it looked like the wing of a raven in flight.

"Comfort Risby? Your housekeeper?"

"Yes, did you write and say ...."

She shook her head.

"I cannot write, or read either. Why should I need to?"

And then she was gone, the broken wooden door closing slowly behind her. I turned for home, frozen through and thoroughly out of countenance. It had been like having a conversation with a child, or someone who was a little simple, yet I knew full well that Tana was neither a child nor simple. I had no idea what her age was, although I thought she was older than I. There was a certain timeless quality about her which ignored the passing of the years.

"I met Tana," I said to Comfort later when she was serving dinner. Now and then Comfort liked to dish up the meal herself, to make sure that everything was in order. "She is very beautiful."

"That's as may be." Comfort put a Sèvres vegetable dish down with rather more force than was good for its safety. "I told you she was a slut, didn't I?"

"You did, but I think you're wrong." I helped myself to redcurrant jelly to eat with the saddle of mutton. "I did not see her in that way."

"Then how?"

I opened my mouth to answer, and then found that I had nothing to say. On reflection, I really did not know what to make of Tana, nor how to describe my feelings towards her. It was only when Comfort had stumped off to the kitchen again that I remembered one thing which Tana had said, and I paused, salt-spoon in mid-air.

"Don't worry," she had said. "Perhaps nothing will happen to you."

I put the tiny spoon down quickly before I spilled its contents. What if Tana's somewhat airy reassurance was misplaced? What if something did happen to me? She must have had some idea of what fate could befall me, if she proved wrong, but what could it possibly be?

Comfort thought I was slightly mad to call on the Cobbs at Heron's Cottage, but I soon dismissed her objections. By now, I had met most of the villagers. They were ordinary enough folk, but the kind that kept themselves to themselves. I was not one of them, and so a speculative look and a moderately civil reply was all I got from them, but I told myself that they might come to accept me in time.

Only the Cobbs had escaped my scrutiny. From what Comfort had told me of them, it seemed unlikely that either Isaac or Annie would have written that note, but it was possible that Annie, at least, might qualify for the role of the unknown witch, and I wanted to assess that likelihood for myself.

I was admitted to the cottage by a grudging Isaac. He glared at me angrily, as if he would have liked to shut the door in my face, but then Annie appeared. She was rosy-cheeked and round like a dumpling, and she pushed her husband out of the way to let me in.

"You be welcome, Miss Lindfield," she said, wiping her hands on her apron. "Come you in and sit down."

I found the tiny living-room crammed with children. They seemed to be of all ages, shapes and sizes, none of them looking much like Isaac, or Annie either for that matter. Lucas was fourteen, and then came Ada, a year younger. Gideon was twelve, Isobel eleven, and Matthew ten. After that there was Matilda aged nine, Jonas six, Adeline five, and two shapeless bundles of two years and six months respectively. Isaac had certainly been busy.

I murmured my greeting to their blank faces, which became rather more animated when I produced bars of chocolate which I had brought with me from Bristol.

"Well, and what do you think of Barley Farm, Miss?"

I perched precariously on a wooden chair which had one leg shorter than the other, and waited for Mrs. Cobb to sink into the rocker on the other side of the worn hearthrug.

"It is very large." I was not sure what to say, but that was a fairly safe beginning. "I was surprised to find it so big."

"Aye, it's big right enough."

"Too big for one." Isaac's small eyes were hostile. "Foolhardy to open it up again."

"Mind your tongue, Isaac Cobb," said Annie tartly. "T'aint none of your business what mistress does with 'er own house."

"I just said. . . ."

"Then don't, for, like I says, it's nought to do with you."

Isaac glowered at Annie and then at me, the children staring at all of us as they sucked away at their rare and unexpected treat.

The conversation seemed to have expired at Annie's sharpness, and I stole a quick look round.

It was all very shabby and none too clean, and I felt a qualm as I remembered that Annie Cobb was responsible for the baking of the bread we ate. I wondered whether she kneaded the dough on the stained wooden table under the grimy window, shuddering at the mere possibility and determining to do without my morning toast in future.

However, my fears were soon put to rest, for Annie invited me to inspect the barn which adjoined the cottage, and there I found the bakery as neat and clean as anything I had seen. She beamed at my praise, and wrapped up two hot rolls in a spotless cloth, pressing them upon me and refusing payment.

"You've been here a long time, I expect." I began cautiously, so as not to drive her into silence. "All your life?"

"Aye, all our lives, me and Isaac. We're Marsh folk, right enough."

"You knew Mrs. Martineau then?"

Annie sighed. "Yes, poor woman, that I did."

"And . . . Mrs. Copper?"

Mrs. Cobb turned away to cover the remaining rolls, so that I could no longer see her face, but she answered calmly enough.

"Her too."

"It was a dreadful thing."

"That it was, but she got her just deserts."

"If she was guilty."

Annie looked back. I caught a flash of something in her eyes, but it was too fleeting to analyse.

"She were."

"Of the murder?"

"What else?"

It was a dead end, so I tried something else.

"I had no idea that when I got here I should find we had a witch in Haydore, Mrs. Cobb. I confess I am quite nervous about the prospect, but perhaps you think it is nothing but an old wives' tale."

She considered me for a moment, brushing flour from her fingers.

"There's a witch, Miss. Don't know who, of course, but there is one."

"But . . . but how can you be so sure?"

She chuckled, her previous reservation gone.

"I'm sure, but never you worry your head about it. Don't suppose he or she will bother you. Let the witch be, and you'll be all right. Don't do to offend, you see, like some have done in the past."

Her eyes locked with mine. I knew what she meant, and she knew that I knew, but there was nothing more to say, and so I took my leave.

I was quite sure that neither Isaac nor Annie Cobb could read or write, and thus I had not bothered to ask them about Comfort's letter, but one thing was certain. Annie had obviously agreed with the anonymous letter-writer. Mrs. Copper had offended someone . . . or something . . . and had paid the price for it.

Later that day I wandered into Mrs. Martineau's sewing-room. There were still reels of cotton and spools of embroidery thread in the marquetry box by her low-backed chair, and in a work-basket I found a half-finished antimacassar with a faded pink rose, worked in wool.

Despite the cold I lingered for a while, deciding that I would order a fire on the following day to warm the room. Comfort would think it an extravagance, but this part of the house needed to be brought to life again with more light and burning coals in the grates.

I noticed that I had left one of the cupboard doors ajar, and was crossing the room to close it when the moaning began. I almost jumped out of my skin, not sure whether to run or cry out for help. I did neither, for my legs would not move and my tongue seemed stuck to the roof of my mouth.

The moaning started again, deep at first, then rising in a cadence of pain. I managed to turn round, afraid that whatever it was which was creating the noise was creeping up behind me, but in the dim light there was nothing there. I told myself it was the wind whistling across the Marshes and finding its way through cracks and crevices of the house, but I knew that it wasn't. It was too eerie for that; even the Romney Marshes could not produce a wind with such terror in its voice.

I slammed the cupboard door shut and got back to the hall somehow, leaning against the wall to recover myself before I encountered Emily or Comfort. I did not want either of them to think me a complete ninny. Perhaps later, when I could trust my voice not to quaver, I would ask Comfort if she had ever heard anything in the sewing-room. I straightened up abruptly, aware of a shadow on the far wall. It was roughly in the shape of a human body, yet so large in size that I had to put my hand over my mouth to stop myself from screaming.

I swung round quickly, expecting to find one of the maids with an oil-lamp, responsible for the optical illusion, but there was no one there. The hall was quite empty. When I looked back, the shadow had gone, and I glanced up at the darkening staircase in the direction of my father's portrait. What would he have thought of me, behaving like a scared child?

I gritted my teeth and walked into the sitting-room, ringing the bell for tea with commendable calm. I would not mention either the moans or the shadow to Comfort.

My father might have been a rake, born out of time, but he was no coward. He should have no cause to be ashamed of me on that score. I would not be a coward either.

FOUR

It was snowing the next morning. I watched the blizzard from my bedroom window and pulled a face. No walk to-day: instead I would continue my detailed inspection of the house, particularly the older part. I refused to let myself think of the events of the afternoon before, and when I had had breakfast, I made my way to Mrs. Martineau's sanctum.

There were no noises here, and at my request a fire had been lit. It was still chilly and I was glad of my shawl, but I soon forgot any discomfort as I picked up ornaments and looked at them, and opened the bureau again to see if there was something in it which would tell me more about the late mistress of Barley Farm.

The letters gave few clues; the bills less still. But then, as I was reaching for a thick envelope in one pigeon-hole there was a sudden click and one of the small panels, which I had thought to be solid, slid back to reveal a cavity. Secret drawers and compartments in desks were nothing new, but the sight of the leather-bound book made my heart leap in anticipation.

It was a diary, inscribed on the first page as Alicia Martineau's journal. Engrossed, I turned the pages. The writing was thin, with curling, spidery loops; careful and precise. Most of the daily entries concerned humdrum details of the household routine.

"To-day, Ada broke my best tea-pot. I shall stop at least

three weeks' wages, the careless girl." "The plums are ripe; to-morrow the jam must be made."

I flicked over more leaves, about to close the diary, when at the end I saw something which made me pause. The script looked shakier than before, and the last two entries were wholly foreign to the previous domestic trivia.

"Oh God, what shall I do? What I think is happening cannot really be true, yet what other explanation is there?" There was a week of silence from Alicia's pen : then the last entry. "It is true, and my mind is stunned, my heart torn in two."

After that there was nothing. Slowly I put the diary back into its place and found the catch which closed the panel. What could have happened? Had the unfortunate Mrs. Martineau discovered that her husband was being unfaithful to her? What else could have caused such anguish to a conventional housewife, who normally wrote only of smashed china and jam-making? Could it have had something to do with her death, for the last entry was dated only a month before that unhappy event?

I left the room, somehow saddened by what I had read. I had the most absurd desire to help Alicia Martineau; to try to drive away her sorrow, but, of course, it was too late. Alicia had died a long time ago.

I went up to the bedrooms, but they contained nothing of interest, and was on the point of making my way downstairs again when I saw a door I had not noticed before. When I opened it I found a flight of stairs in front of me, surprised, because I had not realised that there was an attic in this part of Barley Farm. I needed a lamp, for it was quite dark, and having fetched one from the landing, went up to find myself in a low-ceilinged room with slits of windows, and cupboards round the wall. It had obviously been a nursery, for there was a wooden rocking horse, its dappled splendour dimmed with age and damp; two or three wax dolls in crumbling cotton frocks, a hoop, and a musical box which still managed to tinkle out a few pathetic notes when I touched it.

There was a doll's-house with a broken door, a few books, and a number of trunks and valises. A carpet was rolled up in the corner, and there was even a bird-cage. Unwanted household goods had encroached upon the nursery until only traces of it were left. I wondered what Silas Martineau's daughter had been like, and how she had spent her hours up here before she grew old enough to quarrel with her father and then run away.

Idly, I opened a cupboard in one corner, avoiding the shower of dust. There were a few more items indicating a small girl had once played here, but then I noticed a box on the floor and bent to pick something out of it, perplexed by my find. It was a lead soldier, chipped and slightly bent, and when I dived into the box again I found he had several fellows. There was also a broken bow with some rusted arrows, a tarnished drum, a kite, a whistle and a top.

I rose and brushed by fingers together. Why should there be such toys in a girl's nursery? Silas had had no son. I considered the possibility that his daughter had been a tom-boy, and had liked lead soldiers as much as dolls, but somehow this was not convincing. A companion, perhaps? But why should his belongings be here? Then I stooped down again and saw the boot and the remains of a top of a sailor's suit. They could not possibly have belonged to Silas's daughter, so whose were they?

I went to the kitchen and announced my find to Comfort. Mrs. Bocking was supervising the preparation of vegetables for lunch, hardly looking up as I went in. Louisa's pinched face, with its rather alarming eye, turned in my direction, but apart from a quick glance, neither Agnes Stoop nor Emily, busy cleaning silver, paid much attention to me.

Comfort did not think my discovery either startling or particularly interesting, and I felt somewhat deflated. However, she promised to come and look when she had finished what she was doing, and so I possessed my soul in patience for another hour until she collected me from the sitting-room.

"My what dust!" Comfort was more concerned with the state of the attic than with the worn-out toys. "I must get those girls up here soon to put this right."

"No hurry." Somehow I was anxious that things should be left as they were for a while. "Look, Comfort, in here."

She considered the contents of the cupboard for a minute or two and then turned to look at my face, which I am sure had lost all its colour.

"I don't understand, Miss Charis," she said finally. "There aren't no boys' things here, and certainly no shoe and such."

She was right. My frantic scrabbling in the box and along the shelves proved it, and I stood up and gave a nervous laugh.

"But how extraordinary. They were there, I swear it."

"Not there now." She turned to go, her thoughts back with the luncheon. "Don't worry about it. Easy to mistake one old toy for another, seeing as how they're all covered in dirt, and the light's not too good."

"But the boot and the sailor's suit?"

She shrugged them off too, and began to make her way downstairs again. I wanted to shout to her to stop, and really listen to what I was saying, but I did not want to make a fool of myself. Could I have been mistaken? If there really had been lead soldiers and a boy's boot, surely they would still be there now.

When we got to the passage leading to the main house, we

heard the church bell toll again; softly, insistently, making us listen to it.

"Oh dear, more evil spirits." I tried to joke. "I wonder who does ring it."

Comfort didn't reply, for she was on her way back to the kitchen, and reluctantly I went into the sitting-room to think. I might have accepted Comfort's conclusions about the toys, had it not been for Alicia Martineau's diary. Why I should imagine the two things were in any way connected, I do not know, but two small mysteries, added to all the other odd things, was one too many. Dust or no dust, poor light or not, there had been some boy's things in that attic, and now they were gone.

The first thing which I did was to question the servants. Mrs. Bocking and her daughter Emily denied flatly ever having heard of a boy at Barley Farm. Agnes Stoop shook her head too, but she would have been too young to have known, and Louisa Cockie was not a Haydore girl.

"Never no boy here," said Mrs. Bocking firmly. "Just the one girl, Laura."

"But those things. Were they hers? Why should she have a boy's boot and a sailor's suit?"

When she didn't reply, I knew that she had not accepted the existence of the things at all, and I left the kitchen knowing that she and Emily would be shrugging at one another as if I were not quite right in the head.

But I was not deterred. Why they should lie about such a thing I had no idea, yet I was convinced that my eyes had not deceived me, and so I decided to ask a few other people whether they had known of a young boy connected with Barley Farm. Rather rashly, I started with Dion Mallory.

Probably I should have left him until last, had I not felt his absence from Haydore for so many years made him less likely to side with the villagers.

I made Comfort come with me, and very unhappy about it she was, but I would brook no argument. Still grumbling, she got her bonnet and cape and followed me along the road to Mortdyke.

Bel Rolfe had told me something about the house when he had been talking of the village. It seemed that it dated back to the thirteenth century and had once been a priory. Then it fell into the rapacious hands of Henry VIII's agents, and finally had been sold to one of Mr. Mallory's distant ancestors.

We were admitted by a man-servant, immaculately garbed and extremely surprised to see us. He shewed us through a vast cavern of a hall and into a large room with a painted ceiling and imposing stone pillars at one end. Although there was a roaring fire, it was still draughty, and I hoped that Dion Mallory would not take too long to appear. In fact, he kept us waiting a good five minutes, deliberately I suspected, during which time I had ample opportunity to inspect the beauty of the old, carved furniture and the more modern chairs and thick pile carpet.

When he finally arrived, Comfort retreated discreetly to the far end of the room. Sardonically he watched her go, and then said softly:

"So, this time you have come to call upon me. I said that our next meeting would be inevitable."

"So you did." I refused to be put down by his tone, sitting in the chair he indicated and keeping my back very erect. This was no time to relax. "You will think it strange that I have come."

"Not at all." He sank into another chair and eyed me up and

65

down. "Why shouldn't you call? It is a habit one's neighbours have."

"But not in Haydore."

"No, not normally, so it makes a change."

I noticed that he did not say the change was a pleasant one, and said stiffly :

"This is not a social call, Mr. Mallory. I have come to ask you something."

"I see." The grey eyes seemed to me to grow more watchful, but perhaps I was wrong. "And what is that, pray?"

I went straight to the point, seeing no advantage in skirting round the subject. I told him of my find, the disappearance of the boot and toys, and then said firmly :

"So what I want to know is whether there was a boy at Barley Farm some years ago."

"My dear Miss Lindfield." His voice was a drawl, and I felt irritation prick through me again. "Your servants say no, and they were in Haydore when the Martineaus occupied the house. They knew them, and their daughter. If there had been a boy, why should they not admit it? Besides. . . ." The thin black brows rose slightly. ". . . . did you not say that when your housekeeper went to look, the things had gone?"

"Yes, but I saw them."

"Really?" It was a question and yet not a question. "Are you sure? If they were truly there, what happened to them?"

"I have no idea," I returned shortly. "Mr. Mallory, forgive me for pressing you, but are you certain that you never heard of such a boy?"

"Quite certain." He was uncompromising. "I presume you are speaking of some eighteen or twenty years ago, when Martineau's daughter was a child. I was often at Mortdyke during the holidays at that period. I would have known if there had been a boy at Barley Farm."

"Or even a boy who played with Laura?"

"Laura?"

"That was the name of Martineau's daughter. I am surprised you do not know that, since you were here now and then when she was a child."

"I had forgotten her name." He was smooth, unruffled by my comment. "You asked about a companion. I don't recall one. Certainly she would not have been allowed to mix with the village lads."

"No, I'm sure she wouldn't, and that is why I am so certain it was a different kind of boy."

"Does it matter?" Mallory drew a cigar-case from his pocket. "Do you mind if I smoke?"

"No, of course not, and, yes, it does matter, at least to me."

"I wonder why." He watched a streak of blue haze curl upwards. "Why should you evince such interest in what happened at Barley Farm twenty years ago?"

Without telling him about Alicia's diary, the letter concerning Mrs. Copper, and the other unaccountable things which had happened since I had arrived, his enquiry was difficult to answer.

"I am not sure." I put a bold face on it, trying to pretend his mouth was not curving in a slightly caustic smile. "I just wanted to know, that is all. Did you ever play with Laura?"

"No, I did not." I saw the harshness in his face I had noticed at our first meeting. "I regret that I cannot help you."

"But you knew the Martineaus?"

"I was aware of them, but our paths did not cross very much."

"And Mrs. Copper?"

He turned to flick ash into the grate, but when he looked

67

back his face was bland as before, the trace of anger gone.
"Certainly."

"Do you think she killed Mrs. Martineau?"

Suddenly there was a sharper note in his voice.

"Is there any doubt in your mind about that?"

I was cornered; trapped by my own questions and desire to
keep my secrets.

"No . . . no . . . I suppose not. I just wondered."

"She had a fair trial." He lay back in his chair, totally at
ease. "The stuff was found in her room."

"Yes, I know, but she did not admit to killing her mistress,
did she?"

"How busy you have been." The sneer was gentle but un-
mistakable. "No, she didn't, but that is hardly surprising."

He was silent for a moment. Then he said abruptly:

"May I give you a word of advice? You are a stranger here,
and the natives don't like strangers. The Marshes breed a
special kind of creature and they do not like intruders. You
will find yourself unpopular if you keep asking questions, particularly about something which happened ten years or more
ago. If you want to live here in peace, Miss Lindfield, let
sleeping dogs lie. The dead do not like to be disturbed: the
living like it even less."

To get the taste of Dion Mallory out of my mouth, and his
last remark which had sounded to me very much like a threat,
I decided to call upon Bel Rolfe on the way home. I knew
he would be glad to see me, for he had said he needed company, and he might know something of my mysterious boy.

Before we could reach his house, however, Comfort and I
came upon Henry Jones, and I decided that, there being no
time like the present, to see what he had to say.

He glared at me with positive dislike, as if I had said something indecent, shaking his tousled head vigorously.

"No, no, I know nothing about Barley Farm or who lived there. I told you, I have only been here a few months."

"So you did," I replied sweetly. "Studying birds, was it not, Mr. Jones?"

He flushed, ugly patches standing out on his cheeks.

"Yes, it was. I am going to write a book. Now, if there is nothing else, I must go."

"You ought not to keep asking such things," said Comfort as she watched Henry hasten off. "You'll offend people, see if you don't. I told you afore we got here that you'd get nothing out of the Marsh folk."

"Mr. Jones is not Marsh folk; he's only just arrived. Neither is Dion Mallory, at least, not proper Marsh folk. And you won't stop me, Comfort, so don't even try."

"Bad enough asking about poor Mrs. Martineau," she went on glumly, as if I hadn't spoken, "but when you begin asking about things that weren't even here. . . ."

"They were there," I said stubbornly. "I can't explain what happened to them, but I know they were there. Ring the bell, and let us see what Mr. Rolfe has to say."

While Comfort went to see Jonet in the kitchen, I told my tale once more, this time with more optimism. Bel listened without interruption, his handsome face puzzled by what he was hearing. In the end, he said slowly:

"There was never a boy there as far as I know. Laura, certainly, but no one else. I would have known if there had been for, as you know, I've been here since I was born."

"But how can one account for the toys and that boot?"

He sighed very softly, pausing as if choosing his words with care.

"I don't know that one can, unless. . . ."

"Unless I was mistaken?" I bit my lip. "That's what Comfort says. She's sure I dreamt the whole thing."

"I doubt that." His smile made my frown lift for a moment. "You are too sensible, yet you say that it was dark up there in the attic?"

"Yes, but. . . ."

"And that the things were covered with dust?"

"Yes they were, but. . . ."

"You might have mistaken what you saw, and when you and Comfort returned with more lights, you might have seen what the objects really were."

"But I had a lamp the first time." I could not let it go that easily. "It was not totally dark."

"The next time you had two lamps."

He was laughing with me, not at me, and I could not take offence. In any event it was clear he thought me wrong, and there was no point in going on. As Bel had said, he had lived there all his life; if my boy had existed, he would have known him. I tried to convince myself it was the easiest thing in the world to mistake a bow and arrow for something else, but without success.

Bel offered me tea, but I wanted to go, and so he rang for Jonet. She came in bent and wrinkled as ever, shooting me what seemed a malignant look. I told myself not to be so foolish, but she really was rather a terrifying old thing.

"You must think it a small miracle that Jonet hears me when I ring," said Bel as he rose to his feet. "I will let you into the secret. There is a white ribbon attached to the bell in the kitchen, so that she sees it move. Like all mysteries, so simple when one knows the solution."

I sent Comfort back to Barley Farm, for I had one more

visit to make. She wanted me to go with her, but I refused, almost sharply, and was sorry for my impatience as soon as she was out of sight.

Tana opened the door of the shack in answer to my knock. She did not seem in the least surprised to see me, but stood back to let me in as if my arrival was the most ordinary occurrence.

I told my story yet again. It sounded thinner than ever this time, and, as I expected, Tana shook her head.

"No, I knew no boy. There wasn't one."

"You are sure, Tana. You couldn't be mistaken?"

"Not about that. Sit down and I'll get you a cordial."

I hesitated, but not wishing to appear rude I took a seat next to the old table running through the centre of the room. The shack was totally without heating, and I could feel myself quaking, wondering why on earth Tana did not get pneumonia or worse. She moved gracefully away from me and I looked round. There wasn't much there.

Apart from the table and the bench on which I was sitting, there was only a truckle bed in one corner, two stools, and some cooking pots. I could not think why Tana needed those, since she had no fire, but then my eye lit on the knife hanging on the wall, and the shiver grew deeper. It was long, with a thin polished blade. Whatever would Tana want with such a thing?

I had no time for further pondering because she was back with a handful of apples and cordial in an earthenware cup.

"Have an apple." She motioned me to take one from the table. "I love apples. I could live on them, and almost do." She bit into one, crunching with enjoyment as she perched herself on the edge of the table. "Drink your cordial, it will do you good. Made from wild flowers and other things."

71

She watched me inspect the amber liquid, highly amused at my reaction. Unable to avoid it, I took one gingerly sip and found it surprisingly good. She nodded.

"I drink a lot of that, with my apples."

"How do you cook in here, Tana, and aren't you cold without a fire?"

"Cold?" She looked amazed. "Oh no, I'm never cold. I don't cook either."

"But what do you eat, apart from apples, I mean?"

"Potatoes and greens; a turnip now and then."

"Not raw!"

She laughed aloud at my consternation.

"Of course; they are better that way. What else did you want to ask me, pretty Charis?"

I could not think why she addressed me so, but decided to accept the compliment at its face value.

"Nothing. Only about the boy."

"There wasn't one. Just Laura."

"Then I must go. Forgive me for disturbing you."

"You don't disturb me."

She walked with me to the door, and all at once I thought I smelt a strong perfume. I was startled. A girl like Tana, living on raw vegetables, clad in near-rags, wearing perfume?

The door closed behind me, and I lifted my face up to the snowflakes which had begun to fall thick and fast. More delusions, of course. I was letting the atmosphere of Barley Farm, and its history, get the better of me. Of course Tana did not wear perfume, and, as everyone had insisted, there never was a boy.

I had accepted my over-active imagination and everyone's assurance about the non-existent child, yet the attic where I had seen those things, or rather thought I had, still held some hypnotic attraction for me.

That afternoon I went back, with a large oil-lamp, to have another look round. Fortunately, Comfort had not had time to start cleaning the room, and it was just as I had seen it before. I looked at the toys again; made the rocking horse creak rustily on its hinges, and then went over to the window seat. The wood was split in places, shrivelling up with age. I was about to turn away when I saw something yellowish stuffed into one of the cracks. Quickly I put the lamp down and tried to pull the paper free. It was too firmly stuck, and so I looked round for something to help me. An old poker nearby served the purpose well, and although I splintered part of the seat with the roughness of my hand, I soon pulled free a small bundle of letters, neatly tied with a faded ribbon.

Regardless of the icy draught blowing through the gaps in the windows, I sat down and opened the first letter. As I started to read, I could feel my mouth open in disbelief, my hands unsteady with shock.

It began without preamble or warning of what was to come.

"I can still feel the smoothness of your skin. I think feeling is much more exciting than smelling or seeing, don't you? It was like being part of your body when we lay in bed together. I could not tell whether I was you, or you me. How wonderful it was when we did what we had seen that girl and man do in the barn the other day. Shall we do it again to-morrow?"

Somehow I unfolded the second letter, obviously an answer to the first.

"I love you, I love you, I love you. If you were to go away, I should die. If you tired of me, I would kill you, or myself. Myself, I expect, because there would be nothing left. You are so strong. When you grow to be a man, you will be stronger

73

still, and then I may die anyway because I shall be so happy when you hold me against you. I am so glad that you are beautiful; I hate ugliness. I am beautiful too, don't you think? My breasts are rather small, I know, but they are growing larger, and I shall soon be a real woman, won't I? What joy then for us. Oh, I want to feel you inside me again . . . soon . . . soon . . . soon."

I could not read any more; not then. I folded the two notes up as quickly as my fumbling hands would let me, conscious of several things all at once.

First, the letters had been written by children. It was explicit in what was said, and equally obvious by the immaturity of the old-fashioned script. Not infants, of course, but children of perhaps twelve or fourteen.

Secondly, they had made love. Not just shy nudgings and whisperings and holding hands; these two had made love in the fullest sense of the word.

Thirdly, the notes were written by two young people, well-educated, and not by any village youth or lass. The punctuation was accurate, as was the spelling, and the knowledge revealed was frighteningly adult. There was something raw and totally compelling about the love they confessed for one another; a feeling so deep that they had had to commit it to paper.

But who had they been? Laura? Surely not. For a second I considered whether it was this which had made Mrs. Martineau agonize in her journal, but then I shook my head. No, it could not be that. By the time those last two entries were written, Laura would have been eighteen years old or more. These letters were written by a girl and boy much younger than that.

If not Laura, then who? Or, if it had been Laura, many years before, who was her . . . her lover? I boggled at the word, for it seemed abhorrent to think of a mere child in those terms, yet undoubtedly lovers they had been.

The boy! My heart began to beat faster. Of course, that was it. The boy who everyone said had not existed. Now I knew that they were wrong, or not telling the truth, for it was obvious. There had been a male child. One who played with the broken bow and arrow and toy soldiers and then . . . then made love to a girl whose skin he had found so smooth to touch.

I felt unclean, and got up unsteadily, taking the letters back to my room, where I hid them under the corner of the carpet. I would not let them disappear like the rest of the things, although whether I would have the courage to shew them to Comfort I did not know.

However, after dinner I had regained some of my composure, and asked her if she would come to my bedroom later on because I had found some letters which I wanted her to see. Towards nine o'clock she arrived, and began to turn down the bed.

"Well, Miss Charis?"

I wasn't sure how to begin. Comfort looked so wholesome and ordinary in her black silk and white apron, a streamer of starched linen falling from the cap on her brown hair. Good food had fattened her up, and it suited her; there was fresh colour back into her cheeks. Seeing her enquiring gaze on me I plunged in without stopping to think any more. Too much thought would surely have paralysed my tongue.

Comfort's brown eyes were shocked, cheeks a deeper pink. "Well, really!"

She was outraged, as I knew she would be, yet outraged or not, Comfort would have to see the notes, or she would think I had imagined those as well. I went to the corner of the room and lifted the carpet, feeling the world spin round me as I stared down. The letters had gone.

"What is it?" Comfort was hurrying to my side, seeing my distress. "What is wrong, Miss Charis?"

"They're not here, Comfort. The letters have gone."

She helped me to my feet, clucking as she felt me trembling.

"Now, now, don't take on so," she ordered, and settled me by the fire. "Not like you to get worked up about such things."

"No." I was clenching my hands together in an effort to regain my self-control. "It isn't, is it? But this is different. I don't understand what is happening. Twice I have found things, and twice when I have tried to shew them to you, they have gone. It is as if someone . . . or something . . . is watching me, and when my back is turned it comes and takes the things away."

"Now, now, that's foolish." Comfort was paler now too, but her hand was warm on my shoulder. "It's this place. I said it were wrong to come, what with what happened and all. Shall we go back to Bristol?"

"No, no, of course not." I was glad that I had not told Comfort the real contents of the notes, merely describing them as love-letters. That had disturbed her enough; if she had really known what was in them, I dread to think what she would have said. Perhaps it was just as well that they had gone. "No, we shall stay here. I must be tired. That's what it is."

I knew I wasn't, but this was no time to get hysterical and insist upon my story. I had no evidence now, and I would have to wait to get more, if more there was.

Comfort helped me to undress. I really was rather sleepy after all, and made for the bed, quite ready for the warmth of the featherbed. Then I heard the sound of horses, and turned quickly.

"Comfort! Do you hear that? Those are horses."

I began to move towards the window, but Comfort was there first, standing in front of me and blocking my way.

"No!" She was very firm, her lips clamped together. "No, Miss Charis, don't you look. For God's sake, don't you look. It isn't safe. Come away now do, for if you won't, it'll be the death of you."

FIVE

I made my way down to breakfast the next morning determined to forget all that had happened. I gave the portrait of
my father my usual nod of greeting, and went into the parlour
where Emily was waiting with boiled eggs and hot coffee.

I had been very rational overnight. I had weighed carefully
all the facts and evidence, together with what were probably
some fancies on my part, and had reached the conclusion that
I would be wise to take Comfort's advice and let well alone.

Whatever the circumstances of Alicia Martineau's death,
or that of Mrs. Copper's guilt or innocence, there was nothing
I could do about it now. Obviously I had been wrong about
the presence of a boy at Barley Farm years before. There was
probably some quite simple explanation for what I had seen,
or thought I had seen, and no reason at all why everyone in
Haydore should lie about the existence of such a child.

Alicia's journal was sad, it was true, but no doubt those few
tortured sentences referred to some quite minor domestic up-
heaval, and not the dramatic kind of event I had tried to
picture.

That only left the missing letters, the noises, and the shadow.
The noises and the shadow were firmly put aside. I had been
predisposed to see phantoms in Barley Farm, and so my nerves
had provided them for me. The letters were harder to dismiss,
but I managed to blot them out of my mind too, for, like

everything else from the past, it was none of my affair. They could well have been written many years before Silas Martineau had been master of the house, by two precocious youngsters of another era. The floorboards in my bedroom were far from even; in my hurry to conceal the notes I might easily have thrust them through a gap between two of the shrinking boards.

I even smiled at the thought of the witch. As Bel Rolfe had said : every village had to have something, and we had a witch.

The only thing which I did not quite reject as nonsense was the sound of the horses on the previous night. Perhaps they had been Excise men; perhaps not. But, again, if an odd bottle or two of brandy was being brought through Haydore, it was not my concern.

My good intentions lasted right through that day. I went walking, despite a flurry or two of snow, and then I read some of old Silas's books, which proved a good deal more interesting than Aunt Lavender's had been. I started a piece of embroidery, annoyed when I found I had forgotten to bring any brown silks with me. Then I remembered Alicia's work-box and went off to see what I could find.

It was eight o'clock. I noticed that by the long clock in the hall. It was very dark, but my lamp lit my way through the narrow passage into the old part of the house and thus to the sewing-room. I had just put it down on the table when I heard a woman's cry. It was faint, yet filled with a fear which could not be ignored. I picked up the lamp again and ran back to the kitchen, thinking to find that Comfort or one of the others had met with a mishap. They were sitting round the fire sewing; only Louisa Cockie busy at work making them cocoa.

They all looked up in surprise, and Comfort said quickly :

"What is it, Miss Charis? Is something wrong?"

I took a deep breath, knowing what to look for in their eyes when I told them what I had heard.

"Didn't you hear it?"

"Hear what?" Comfort put her work down and stood up. "I heard nothing. What was it?"

"A woman's cry." I was right. They were all patently sceptical. "I heard a woman cry out, as if she were very frightened. I thought perhaps it was one of you."

"Not us, Miss." Emily Bocking exchanged a look with her mother. "We heard nothing."

"I'm sorry to have disturbed you." I would not let Ellen's pallid gaze disconcert me. "I just thought...."

"A Marsh bird, like as not." Emily went back to her sewing. "Funny noises them things make."

"Yes ... yes, of course."

I made as dignified an exit as possible, sure that they were either laughing at me or shaking their heads at my eccentricity. I could not face the sewing-room again that night, and so I went up to my room. On the stairs I stopped, the lamp unsteady in my hand. The odd creaking noise had started again, clear as ever. I could not return to the kitchen with yet another such tale, so I scurried to my room and sat down in front of the mirror to look at my wan face. It was not an encouraging sight.

I lay in bed, staring at the ceiling, keeping the light on until I felt calmer. At eleven o'clock I decided that it was time that I slept, and was on the point of dousing the lamp when I heard footsteps overhead. They were heavy, like a man's, squeaking loudly over the joists. Grimly I threw back the bedclothes and put on my peignoir. It could only be Comfort or one of the Bockings. I was being a simpleton again. I got to the landing, holding the candle high so that I could see the hall below, feeling my colour seep away again as I saw Comfort, the Bockings, Agnes and Louisa making their last check of doors and windows, and then pass through the green baize door to the back staircase.

None of them could possibly have been upstairs in the attic a minute or two ago; there was no chance for any one of them to have got back to the ground floor by the time I reached the stairwell.

All the things I had resolutely put out of my mind flooded back with a vengeance. The anonymous letter, the state of the furniture after ten years neglect, the mysterious boy, and the passion of those childish love-letters. I rushed back to bed and hid my head under the clothes.

During the next few days the noises increased. First the creaks at night; the rustling, scratching sound on the stairs; even another cry, fainter than before. I kept them all to myself, for I knew no one would believe me. Finally, however, after a particularly noisy night, which no one else seemed to have experienced, I sent Louisa with a note to Dion Mallory.

I do not know why I decided to seek his advice, since he was the most unpleasant person in Haydore, but at the time he seemed the most logical choice. Bel would have been more sympathetic, but his blindness would have made it impossible for him to assist. Besides, Mallory had spent years away from the Marshes and would not be bewitched by them as others might be. Henry Jones was a stranger too, of course, but somehow he did not inspire me with any confidence, and since he seemed to dislike me as much as Dion Mallory did, it might as well be Mallory himself.

"So, Miss Lindfield, you have now started to hear noises. How very distressing for you."

I had dismissed Emily, and poured brandy for him myself,

81

gritting my teeth at his tone. I must not lose my temper with him, for I wanted his help, but he really was a most exasperating man.

"Yes, I have," I replied shortly. "I cannot accept that I am imagining them, but I think that even Comfort Risby is beginning to suspect I am."

I handed him the glass, conscious of a faint whisper of perfume, strong and easily recognisable. Fortunately he was not looking at me, or he would have seen the shock in me. Dion Mallory and Tana? I sat down quickly, keeping my hands still by locking them tightly together. I suppose Tana was just the kind of woman who would attract a man like Mallory : attract any man, for that matter, for she was very lovely. I wanted to feel disgusted with him, but I couldn't. All I could feel was a dull pain, which I did not understand.

I told him about the noises, which no longer seemed quite so important as they had been. He listened, watching me from those clear, direct eyes, giving nothing of his thoughts away.

"Old houses do make noises at night," he said when I had finished. "Rats, creaking furniture and floorboards."

"And the woman's cry?"

"A Marsh bird, as your servant suggested."

"I don't think so, and that is why I asked you to come. The sounds start about this time of night. Will you come into the other part of the house and listen with me?"

"Of course." He was disbelieving, but for once obliging, and we walked through the darkened hall into the sewing-room. From there we went to Mrs. Martineau's sanctum, and even up to the bedrooms, but the silence was absolute.

Back in the sitting-room again, I said hesitantly :

"I have wasted your time, Mr. Mallory, and you must think me feeble-minded."

"Only because you stay here instead of going back to Bristol."

"I won't be driven away by noises."

"Even non-existent ones?"

"Even those," I returned stonily. "There are other things here which need an explanation. I am determined to find out about them."

I turned my head to look at him, chilled by what I read in his face. It was not pity or contempt, but cold anger, barely veiled. Then he rose.

"Take care, Miss Lindfield. You may be dabbling in something beyond your capacity or control. Good-night, and thank you for your hospitality."

I caught another whiff of the scent as he passed by me to the door, trying to thrust away the totally unexpected hurt as Emily shewed him out.

I could not sleep that night. After tossing and turning for what seemed hours, I got up and went to the window, moving the curtains to one side. I froze as I saw the blur of lanterns and the shadowy outline of the horses moving slowly and carefully in the darkness. I could see the direction they were taking, knowing that the windows at the rear of the old part of the house would shew their further passage. Forgetting my fright, I put on my dressing-gown and fled downstairs, armed with a candle. I don't remember getting through the passage to the sewing-room, or up the stairs to the back bedroom, but I must have done so for I found myself peering out of the window, watching the riders out of sight.

I was really quite calm, all things considered, for at last I could see some normal explanation. I was sure the horses had not belonged to the Excise men this time, which meant that they probably belonged to men still carrying on the old smuggling trade. That would make some kind of sense, and account for some of the secrecy which surrounded Haydore. It would not explain everything, of course, but at least there was nothing supernatural about smugglers.

I went down the stairs, still unafraid, and when I saw the door of the powder-closet was open I really thought nothing of it, save that it had blown open in the wind. For some reason I opened it further, holding my candle up.

I know now what is meant by one's hair standing on end, for mine did at that moment. There was a man there, dressed in knee-breeches and brocaded coat, with powdered wig and silver-topped cane in his hand. I let out one scream and fled, spilling hot wax in my terrified flight back to my bedroom.

"You must have been mistaken, Miss Charis," said Comfort the next morning when I told her about it. "Whatever were you doing there at that time of night, anyway?"

"I was not mistaken," I returned tautly. "I could not sleep and I . . . well . . . I was just walking about to . . . to. . . ."

"You'll catch your death of cold." She was severe. "Now, you come with me and we'll see what's in the cupboard which frightened you."

Louisa Cockie was cleaning the stairs when we arrived. She bobbed at me, puzzled as Comfort ordered her aside and opened the door of the powder-closet. I held myself motionless, expecting my apparition to be waiting for us, but all that was there was a dusty wig on a stand, and a faded counterpane draped over a high-backed chair.

"There," said Comfort accusingly. "That's what you saw. That wig on the stand and the bedspread."

I did not argue; it was no good. Comfort had made up her mind, and she left me with another brief lecture on the folly of wandering about the house at the dead of night, clad only in my peignoir.

When she had gone, I looked at Louisa. It was difficult to do so, because of the appalling squint, but I could see the sympathy on her face, and tried to make light of what had happened.

She listened earnestly. Then she said in a whisper :

"I should put a horseshoe by the doorstep, Miss. That's the best thing to do."

"A horseshoe?" I looked at her vacantly, my ghost of the previous night forgotten. "Whatever for, Louisa?"

"They can't cross iron, you see." She was very serious, rubbing away at the banister rail. "They hates iron."

"Who?" I was bewildered. "Louisa, what do you mean? Who hates iron?"

"The witches, Miss. Won't ever cross iron, 'specially a horseshoe."

I was shaken, but I murmured something non-commital and left Louisa to her work. I might have forgotten her words if Comfort had not come to me later that day, her face like whey, something clutched in a hand which was visibly unsteady.

"Comfort, what is it?"

She gave a small shudder.

"It's this, Miss Charis. Oh God, we should leave here now, before it's too late."

"But what is it? Here, let me see it."

I took the small bottle from her, gazing at the yellowish fluid and odd fragments of something floating in it.

"Comfort! Whatever is it? Where did you find it?"

"Louisa found it." She tried to pull herself together. "Over the other side, by that closet. As to what it is . . . well . . . Louisa says it's something . . . something nasty."

"It looks like . . . I don't know. I'm not sure what it looks

85

like."

I was as nervous as Comfort now, but I would not let her see it.

"It's urine, so she says, with nail parings in it. I tried to make her tell me what it meant, but she wouldn't say no more, save that it was to do with the . . . the witch."

"Oh, come!" I tried to dismiss the absurdity, but the horrid notion would not go away. "You don't believe that, do you?"

"No, no, I suppose not, really, yet. . . ."

"Yes?"

"Well, it's odd, like, coming on top of what I heard Ellen say to Emily yesterday."

"What was that?" I put the bottle down hastily. "What did you hear?"

Comfort was restive. Clearly, she could dismiss my tales of noises and figures in closets as nonsense, but the witch was something else.

"I ought not to bother you with such rubbish," she said in a worried tone, "but maybe you ought to be told. Perhaps then you'll see why Barley Farm is no place for us."

"Do go on!" I was impatient. "What did they say?"

"It will soon be Candlemas."

"What about it?" That did not sound very sinister to me, and I took fresh heart. "Why should the thought of Candlemas worry you?"

"They said it was the old Celtic Feast of Imbolc; one of the great Sabbats. 'Course, they didn't know I was listening, or they wouldn't have said so much, but they talked of something which was going to happen in the church on that night."

"But the church is a ruin."

"I know." She gave another shudder. "But that wouldn't stop . . . well . . . if what they say is true, that wouldn't matter, would it?"

I had to throw off my own doubts for Comfort's sake, forgiving her for not taking my experiences seriously, and I was well-pleased with the steadiness of my voice.

"You mean if there was going to be a Sabbat? Comfort, I really think this is too silly." I did not believe what I was saying, for I was staring at the bottle and remembering what Louisa had said about horseshoes. "We are letting our imaginations run away with us. It's my fault for worrying you with my noises and seeing a man who wasn't there. There are no witches. How could there be?"

"Maybe not, and maybe it's nonsense as you say. I thought so at first, till Louisa found that thing. Then there was something else I heard. Not from Ellen and Emily, but something young Louisa had picked up, although she wouldn't tell me how. It seems that that young man what drowned about the same time as Mrs. Martineau died, might not have had an accident."

My mouth dried to dust.

"Not . . . an accident?"

"No. Louisa swears she heard it was murder. He'd offended too, you see."

"She . . . didn't say whom he had offended?"

"She don't know that. Here, Miss, give that to me. I'll do away with it."

When Comfort left me, I tried to put all the pieces of the last two weeks together, but it wasn't easy. No one thing seemed to bear any relation to any other. Were there smugglers? Was that what it was all about? But what could smugglers have to do with Mrs. Copper, or those letters which I had found in the playroom? There could not really be a witch, but was someone in the village trying to make others believe that there was, and, if so, why?

I sat down and thought long and hard about those living in Haydore. Dion Mallory was rich. Had he made his money through contraband? That was possible, but the idea of the aloof Mr. Mallory as a witch was beyond even the wildest of my dreams. Bel could hardly be involved, since he was blind, but Jonet, the deaf mute, looked the nearest thing to a witch I could conjure up. Tana? The wild and exquisite creature who lived on apples and raw vegetables, and made love to Mallory? That was conceivable. Henry Jones? Hardly. He had only recently come to the village, and though he was a surly young man, I did not see him in such a fanciful role, although he might not be above a little bootlegging. Annie and Isaac Cobb; again improbable.

I realised that although I could not really see any of my own servants, or my neighbours, as responsible for what was going on, nor envisage them turning into a witch when the mood was upon them, equally I could not trust any one of them, except Comfort.

I suddenly began to think of Miss Prentiss, who had been Laura Martineau's governess, and who had left the village a few months before without a word of explanation. I wished that she were still here, for she might have been able to tell me something. Perhaps she had been frightened away by someone . . . or something.

There was only one thing to do. I dreaded the thought of it, and was not sure whether I would be able to summon up enough courage to go through with it. I would have to go to the church on Candlemas night and see for myself. I could not ask anyone about the Bockings' conversation, in case that person was involved. I would have to do it alone.

I went up to look at the portrait of my father, willing it to

give me courage. Somehow it did. The painted smile seemed
to me to be more amused than usual, the azure eyes challeng-
ing. He would have expected me to go, and not sit and twitter
by the fireside about things which probably meant nothing at
all, and were merely village rumours and gossip.

I felt easier when my mind was made up. If there was
nothing in the church on Candlemas night, I would have
confirmation that the witch-talk was false, as I had told Comfort. If there was someone there, I should see his, or her, face
with my own eyes, and then I should know where the danger
lay. One way or the other, I had to be sure.

On the second of February I had my hot chocolate at ten
o'clock as usual. Emily brought it in on a small tray and put it
by my side. In the old days, Comfort and I had had to make
do with a mouthful or two of watered milk, for tea was too
expensive for the likes of us, and Aunt Lavender would have
thought chocolate a decadent luxury, even for herself. Now,
I had it each night, savouring it with pleasure, as if it were the
rarest of wines.

I left the cup on the table for Emily to collect and went up
to bed. There must be no deviation from the normal routine;
nothing to alert Comfort to what I proposed to do. I even
undressed and got into bed, so that when she came to bid me
good-night, I was convincingly sleepy in my warm flannel
nightgown.

I waited until eleven-thirty. I knew by then that everyone
would be in their attic bedrooms, and probably snoring soundly
after a hard day's work. Dressing took no time at all, and I
collected a small lamp and some matches and slipped out of
the house by the side door.

There was a pale moon that night, and it made the village

look more sinister than ever. In the darkness one cannot see shapes and shadows. By even the most limpid of moons there are unexplained things to avoid. The wind was coming over the Marshes with its usual whine, blowing angrily at my skirts for daring the venture out at that hour. No one was about; the village had retired long since, and only I was abroad on my fool's errand.

By the time I reached the church, my chief emotion was not fear but a recognition of the ridiculous sight I must have presented, had there been any about to see me. My decision to visit the church at Candlemas had seemed logical enough when I made it; now, I thought I had made a complete idiot of myself for listening to the Bockings' chatter.

As I went through the open doorway I felt a sudden giddiness, holding on to the wall until the moment passed. It was probably a chill coming on, and I had only myself to thank for it. By now, the lantern was alight and I trod warily into the ruin, looking up at what remained of the roof far above me.

It was very silent and, as far as I could tell, there was no movement of any kind. I held the light up so that I could see the watch pinned to my bodice. Ten minutes to go to midnight. The unpleasant dizziness struck me again, and I groped over to a broken pew and held on to its back.

Surely I was not going to faint at such a time as this? I shook my head to clear it, still glad of the support of the rotting wood. It was much easier to believe in witches in the ruins of Haydore Church than it had been at Barley Farm. The darkness and the feel of cobwebs as I moved forward a pace or two heightened the conviction that something must be there.

I began to have a strong sensation of nausea, and my head was swimming again, but I would not let myself turn for the door. Another five minutes, and then I could decently leave and make for my own bed.

When the music first began, I thought it was a noise inside my own head. It was a thin, reedy sound, like that made by pipes or a flute. My skin came up in goose-pimples, but still I would not give way, moving even further into the church until I came to the nave.

I could see some queer marks on the floor, and then realised with a thud of alarm that it was not simply my own modest lantern which was providing light. Here and there, round the walls, other lights had appeared, bobbing and unsteady in the draught coming through the gaping windows. The music had grown louder, and I was sure that I could hear people chanting, but the light-headedness was growing worse, and I forced myself to think that it was that, and not the presence of unseen companions singing in low voices.

I lurched on, seeing the shape of an altar wavering in front of me some distance ahead. It had candles on it, glowing like pin-points of fire, and there was someone dancing in front of it, white limbs twisting and turning.

I almost retched, clutching at another pew as I tried to steady myself, closing my eyes tightly. Who would dance naked in Haydore Church on a freezing February night? It was impossible, yet the figure was still there when I opened my eyes again.

The world was tilting wildly, and I was convinced that I was rising from the ground, floating above it like a disembodied spirit. Hard as I fought to release myself from such a bizarre thought I could not do it, and with every second which passed the music seemed to grow louder, the dancing more feverish.

I thought that someone was calling my name, but I could not be sure because of the music and the sound of rushing water in my ears.

It was then that the smell came: an odour like nothing I had known before. I knew that I had vomited, but it made me feel no better, and the stench was thick in my nostrils and throat, choking me until I felt I had to fight for the very air I needed to survive.

In what seemed to me to be my delirium, fantastic thoughts came to me. Ill though I felt, I wanted to dance too; to tear off my clothes and join the girl ahead of me. I groped forward another step or two, sensing something all round me. I tried to focus, turning first right, then left.

There were others there; just shapes. They were moving in on me from both sides, mouthing my name. I was rooted to the spot now, unable to go forward or run for the door. The candles were blurring, and my eyes were beginning to close, when a bright light sparked quite near to me and jerked me back to near-consciousness.

I only saw the briefest glimpse of a face, and what looked to me for all the world like the horn of a deer, but that could not be. It was as impossible as all the other things which were happening, and I tried to drive them off by shutting my eyes once more.

"Charis."

Someone was calling me; there was no mistake that time. I tried to lift my head, but the effort was almost too much.

"Charis, look at me."

Somehow I raised my head and forced my lids apart, the world crumbling round me as I saw what was in front of me.

"No!"

My small moan was drowned in the noise all about me, and I knew that I had dropped my lantern, wondering inconsequentially whether it would catch my skirt alight.

The figure stretched out a hand, but it wasn't a real hand. It seemed to have skin or fur on it, and there were no proper fingers. I sank down on my knees, cringing away from whatever it was, and then all the confusion and babble and lights vanished as I sank into blessed oblivion.

It was four o'clock in the morning before I regained consciousness. At first, I lay on the floor of the church, my eyes trying to adjust to the darkness. I could not think where I was for a while, believing myself to be in the throes of a nightmare, but then the numbness of my hands and the chill current of air on my face made me sit up abruptly.

The lantern I had brought with me was still burning, perched on a nearby pew. Somehow I got to my feet and looked round. The ruined church was completely empty as far as I could tell, but I had only the haziest recollection of what had happened. When I began to remember, I shook like an old woman, seizing the lamp and holding it up, dreading what I should see. There was nothing there. After my initial paralysis, I became bold enough to inspect the floor, looking for those weird marks. There was only dust, splinters and the remains of a broken lectern and pulpit. I moved on to the east end, but there was no altar decked with candles; simply the tottering frame of what had once been the holy table.

There was no smell, and certainly neither voices nor music. I turned back and went slowly through the west door, totally confused and feeling damp and vastly uncomfortable. I knew that I should have to hurry, because the household would begin to stir at five-thirty, and I did not want to encounter Louisa yawning her way downstairs to scrub the floors, or meet the inquisitive stare of Agnes Stoop on her way to light the fires.

The cold morning breeze was a great restorative, and by the

time I had reached the side door I felt better. I bolted it furtively behind me and crept upstairs, peeling off my clothes and washing myself all over with icy water until I tingled.

I lay down, not expecting to sleep, and began to consider what had happened. My thoughts were disconcerting bedfellows, because I was not at all sure by then that anything had happened at all. If it had, there would have been some sign when I awoke of what I thought I had seen. There had been nothing; not a trace of anybody or anything.

And I had felt ill almost as soon as I had reached the church. The sickness and giddiness could have been the result of something I had eaten. Expecting to see heaven knows what, my upset stomach and pumping head had obligingly produced the necessary illusions for me. There could be no other explanation.

I found that my memory of what I believed I had seen was growing dimmer. Candles, murmuring voices, music. Had they existed? I wasn't sure now. At the back of my mind was a blur concerning something which had stretched out a limb towards me, but the recollection slid away again as quickly as it had come. Then I sat upright in bed, clutching the blankets to me.

I had seen a face; I was sure of that. I wished I could chase that away as easily as I had dismissed the rest of the things I did not want to remember, but I couldn't.

It had been there, I was sure of it. Or was I? I decided that I was not sure. It was a much easier way out than contemplating the reason for Dion Mallory's presence in Haydore Church on Candlemas night.

SIX

I did not wake up the next morning until nearly nine o'clock. Comfort came in with a breakfast tray, full of apologies.

"Emily brought you tea at seven-thirty as usual," she said as she pulled the curtains, "but you was sleeping so sound, she let you be. I would have come sooner myself, but I was that late getting up."

I roused and plumped up the pillows. My head ached and I felt wretched, but it would not do to let Comfort see that.

"It doesn't matter," I said as she settled the tray on my knees. "Why shouldn't you sleep late now and then?"

"Not until eight o'clock." Comfort made it sound like a capital offence. "Right down lazy, that's what it is, but do you know, I simply couldn't get my head off the pillow. Slept like the dead last night, I did."

I regarded her thoughtfully. She didn't look her usual blooming self; rather drawn and peaky. It occurred to me that she might have eaten the same thing I had done, and that we had both suffered from some mild form of food-poisoning. I tapped the top of my boiled egg and thought about the night before, but it was no more than a haze by now.

"What about the others? Are Emily and Ellen all right?"

"They're fine. Ada's sulking 'cos she had a bit of extra work to do, but otherwise there's nought wrong with them." She seemed to notice my face for the first time that morning. "You

95

don't look well, though."

"I think it was something I ate." I hoped she would move away from the bed and not press me too closely. "You too, perhaps."

"Maybe. Perhaps we're not used to such rich food yet. I'll get Mrs. Bocking to cook something plain to-day."

She began to pick up the clothes I had dropped the night before, giving a sudden exclamation.

"Miss Charis! This skirt's wet. So's the cloak."

I was very busy with my toast, not looking up to meet her accusing stare. I had been careless; I should have hidden the offending garments away somewhere, but I had been too tired.

"Are they? I should have hung them up when I came in yesterday afternoon."

Comfort laid the clothes over a chair and came back to the bed.

"You said I never fooled you, Miss Charis. You never fooled me neither. You went out last night, didn't you?"

It was pointless to lie to Comfort, for she was right. We had never been able to fool one another.

"Well, yes, I did."

Her lips compressed.

"And I know where you went too. You went to the church, didn't you?"

I nodded, pushing my plate away.

"Yes. It was stupid of me, I know, but after what the Bockings had said I wanted to see for myself whether there was any truth in their story."

"And was there?"

I did not answer for a while, making the drinking of my second cup of tea an excuse for my silence. I had to decide quickly whether or not I was going to tell Comfort of what remained

of my memories of last night. I would have liked to do
so, just to clear my mind and have her laugh at my fancies,
but I was not sure that she would laugh. Although she had
not believed the stories of the toys and letters, and had
made light of the noises I said I had heard, she was obviously
beginning to worry about the possibility of a witch. That small
bottle hadn't helped, and goodness knows what else the two
Bockings had been saying to her.

"No." I put the cup aside, my mind made up. It wasn't
fair to Comfort to frighten her, particularly about something
which might not have happened at all. I had felt very ill for a
while, and in such a state could have imagined anything.
Besides, when I had awoken, the church had shewn no signs
that it had been peopled with shapeless forms or disturbed by
shrill uncanny music. "No, there was nothing there."

"Thank goodness for that." Comfort was disposed to scold
me now that her fears had been allayed. "Don't you go out
again by yourself at night, Miss Charis. You stay in your own
bed, like the good Christian girl you are."

"Comfort."

"Mm?"

"Do the Bockings ever speak of Miss Prentiss, Laura Martineau's governess?"

"No, not that I can recall. What made you think of her?"

"I don't know. She just came to mind. I wonder why she
ran away."

"We don't know that she actually ran away." Comfort
picked up the tray and made for the door. "Just moved off,
and who can blame her?"

When I had washed and dressed I paused by the window.
Beyond the shrubs and stunted trees in the garden I could see
the Marshes, dim and baleful. It was then that I noticed Henry

Jones stooping over something on the ground. He was some distance away, but easily recognisable by his thatch of hair. He was a peculiar young man, I thought. Not the kind to study birds, and certainly not one to write a book about them. Yet if that was not the true reason, why had he come to Haydore? What else could have brought him to such a place as this? I made up my mind to engage him in conversation again before long, pinning him down in some way so that he could not rush off the minute I began to talk to him.

I met Louisa on the stairs, brushing away diligently.

"Good-morning, Louisa." I thought the child looked scared as I spoke, and that her efforts grew more vigorous, as if she hoped it would drive me away. "You haven't found anything else, have you?"

"What, Miss?"

She was forced to look at me then, the squint more pronounced than ever.

"Found anything," I repeated firmly. "You know, like that bottle."

Her lower lip trembled, and she shook her head.

"No, nothing more."

"Perhaps I ought to have taken your advice and got a horse-shoe," I said lightly. "I'll have to think about it."

"Too late." Louisa turned away again. "Too late now, Miss, the harm's done."

I knew she wouldn't say any more, and so I continued my journey downstairs, frowning over Louisa's words. Too late? I looked back at her when I reached the end of the flight, but there was nothing to see of her but voluminous cotton skirts and heavy boots.

If a witch would not cross iron, and it was now too late to procure a horseshoe to keep one out, there could only be one answer to Louisa's comment. It was too late because the witch was already inside Barley Farm.

I told myself crossly that I was a numskull, and went into the parlour to get on with my embroidery.

I went up to bed at ten that evening. I was still tired and feeling the effects of the previous night, but a good sleep would cure me of my ills. I took a candle from the sitting-room and made my way out into the hall. It was dimly lit, the staircase in almost complete shadow.

I was not feeling nervous: not even expecting the creaking noises which sometimes seemed to hover about the polished wooden steps. If I was thinking of anything at all, it was of Dion Mallory, angered at my dislike of his liaison with Tana.

Thus, when I raised my candle to light my way, I was not prepared for the shock of finding someone on the upper landing. It was a woman, for I could see part of her wide blue skirt and starched linen apron, lifting the candle higher until I saw the neatly-dressed hair, and shawl over thin shoulders.

"Emily?"

My voice was hesitant, for I knew it wasn't Emily. She had blonde hair, whereas the unmoving figure above me was dark. It wasn't Ellen either, and certainly not the squat Agnes Stoop.

I could feel the saliva drain from my mouth, and the holder was quivering in my hand.

"Comfort? Is that you?"

I knew it could not be, of course, but it had to be somebody. The face was turned away from me, but as I managed to mount another stair or two I caught the gleam of a gold ear-ring.

I knew then that I wouldn't have the courage to go any further, but for a moment I could not retreat either. I just stood and stared at the motionless figure, waiting for it to turn or speak. It did neither, and then my candle went out.

I gave a sharp cry and whirled round, almost falling down the stairs as I began to shout for Comfort.

She came, and with her Ellen Bocking, Agnes, with Louisa bringing up the rear.

"For mercy's sake, Miss Charis, what is it?"

Comfort was holding my shaking hands, drawing me into the sitting-room, the others following.

"What is it, love?" She forced me into a chair, and sent Louisa for hot milk. "Did you fall?"

"No! No!"

I could not stop shivering, and Comfort motioned to Agnes to make up the fire.

"Then what was it? Did you hear something again?"

I looked up at their faces. Comfort's full of anxiety and concern; Ellen's wiped of emotion; Agnes's greedy and waiting for some dramatic announcement from me.

"I . . . I . . . saw someone," I said finally, and tried to control the shudder which ran through me. "There was a woman on the landing upstairs."

"A woman?" Comfort frowned. "But there couldn't have been. We was in the kitchen; all of us, 'cept Emily, who was in the pantry."

"I tell you there was a woman." I knew my voice was rising to shrill panic, but I was past caring. "I saw her. I spoke to her."

"What did she say?"

"N . . . nothing. I asked who she was, but she didn't answer."

Louisa arrived with the milk, which I took gratefully, and with her was Emily, wiping her hands on a cloth.

"Sorry, Miss," she said, almost apologetic for once. "I was

100

sorting pickles when I 'eard what happened. One of them bottles was broken and my hands got covered."

"You must have been mistaken." Comfort watched me drinking, and shook her head. "There couldn't have been anyone up there, now could there? See, we're all down here."

"What was she like, Miss; this woman?"

I glanced up at Mrs. Bocking and raised my shoulders helplessly.

"I don't really know. The light was not good, and she was some way away from me. I was afraid to go up any further. She had a blue skirt on and a shawl. She was dark, but her face was turned away from me. Oh, I did notice one thing. She had gold ear-rings . . . at least . . . I saw one gold earring."

There was a frozen silence, and I saw the Bockings exchange a frightened glance.

"What is it?" I asked sharply. "Mrs. Bocking, why do you look like that? Do you know who this woman is?"

"Was, Miss," she replied and shuffled her feet. "Was, you might say."

"Was? What on earth are you talking about? Emily, what does your mother mean? If you know who this woman is, tell me! What is she doing here?"

Emily gave a small nervous cough.

"Mrs. Copper wore blue a lot. She were dark too, and always wore gold ear-rings."

The glass dropped out of my nerveless fingers, and Comfort was ashy as she bent to rescue it.

"Mrs. Copper? Emily! What are you saying? How could it have been Mrs. Copper? She's dead."

"Yes, Miss, but she's been seen before. It were her ghost you saw up there right enough."

Hurriedly, Comfort shooed them from the room, shutting the door firmly behind them.

"Don't do to take no notice of them." She was trying not to let her own teeth chatter. "They'll tell you anything, those two."

"But there was someone there; I saw her. I wasn't mistaken this time, I know it. And Henry Mutton said this house was haunted."

Despite her fears, Comfort said crossly :

"He'd no right to say such things to you. No wonder you hears things and sees things, him putting ideas like that into your head."

"I did see her." I said it wearily, lying back in the chair and wondering how I would have the courage to mount that staircase again. "She was there; I'm certain of it."

But when Comfort had finally got me to bed, promising to sit by my side until I was asleep, I found I wasn't really sure of anything anymore. If there was no such things as ghosts, and how could there possibly be, then perhaps I had been thinking too much of Mrs. Copper and her tragic end.

I would put her right out of my mind, and not think of her again. I turned on my side, squeezing my eyes shut, and fell asleep, thinking of Dion Mallory.

Later that week I went to call on the Cobbs again. I had ordered some more sweetmeats from Elmbrook, and when they arrived I took myself off to Heron's Cottage.

Annie welcomed me in, making up the fire with a few sticks of wood.

"Nice to see you again, Miss," she said in a friendly tone. "Don't get many visitors nowadays."

I glanced round at the children, staring at me, or rather

102

at the packet on my lap. There seemed fewer of them than before, and as I handed out the chocolate and toffee, I made a joke about the diminishing family.

"Yes, that's right." Annie nodded. "Gideon and Matthew be off to stay with their aunt in Lydd."

"They won't come back no more."

I looked up quickly. It was Matilda who had spoken, the solemn nine-year-old, sucking a toffee-bar with great relish.

"What foolishness!" Annie snapped the words out, her previous good-humour entirely gone. "Of course they'll be back. Hold your tongue, unless you want to feel my strap."

"They never come back."

Matilda backed away from the glowering Mrs. Cobb, but she was stubborn in her insistence. Annie tossed her head, finally deciding against physical assault while I was present.

"What ideas them children get," she said grinning again as if nothing had happened. "Little minx only says these things to make folk notice her. Seeing she's not pretty, nor clever either, she has to draw attention to herself somehow. Be off with you!"

She made a threatening but empty gesture in the direction of her brood, who scattered out of the door, just in case my presence was not enough to save them from their mother's wrath. Annie and I talked about the weather, and I praised her bread. Then I said tentatively:

"Mrs. Cobb, did you hear anything unusual on the 2nd February. At night, I mean?"

She plumped herself down opposite me, lifting threadbare skirts to warm her knees.

"Candlemas night, you mean?" Her eyes looked very bright by the flicker of the crackling wood. "No, not that I can recall. What sort of something?"

"Anything."

103

She smiled, and I had the feeling that she was laughing at me for my innocence, but she remained civil enough.

"Nothin' but Isaac's snores. Lord above, how that man can snore."

"And nothing else?"

"No, Miss, nothing else."

As I walked back to Barley Farm I considered the possibility that she had been untruthful. There was no reason why she should be, unless of course . . . I let the idea disperse before it had time to take root. Then I remembered Matilda, in her ragged frock and worn-out boots. Not at all pathetic, but stoutly brave in the face of accepted poverty. I could not imagine why she should think her two brothers would not return, nor what she had meant by saying that they never came back. Annie must have been right : it was just a way of gaining attention. Children were odd little creatures, and in any event one missing boy was quite enough for me.

Dion Mallory came to see me that evening at my request. Comfort hadn't liked my invitation to him, but I had put on my most mistressy air, so that she should not argue with me.

He nodded to me as Emily shewed him into the sitting-room, waiting for her to close the door behind her.

"I am honoured," he said with a faint hint of sarcasm. "Another call from the lovely Miss Lindfield, and so soon. I swear I feel that Haydore may have some future for me yet, if the social life continues to improve so."

I did not rise to the bait.

"Please sit down, Mr. Mallory. This is not a social occasion."

The hard mouth curved.

"I was afraid it might not be. You are not a very sociable person, are you?"

"No, I suppose not. Will you have whisky or brandy?"

"Brandy please, and if you have not summoned me here to make polite conversation with you, what is the reason?"

I poured his drink and sat down before answering. It was difficult to choose the right words, and the tilt of his eyebrow made it no easier.

In the end I abandoned the subtle approach and went straight to the point.

"Were you in Haydore Church on Candlemas night?"

He stared at me as if I had taken leave of my senses, his glass frozen in mid-air.

"In Haydore Church? That ruin? My dear girl, why ever should I be there, on Candlemas night or any other occasion for that matter?"

"Do you swear that you were not?"

He gave me a straight look and said briefly :

"On a stack of Bibles, if that will put your mind at rest. Why do you ask?"

"I thought I saw you there." I glanced down at my hands, feeling ridiculous. His opinion of me had obviously been low before to-night; now he would dismiss me as a complete dolt. "I must have been mistaken."

"This is good brandy." He contemplated its deep colour with approbation, and then looked back at me. "If you thought you saw me there, it follows without question that you were there yourself. Why?"

I told him of the Bockings' conversation, and he gave an exasperated laugh.

"And on the strength of those foolish women's stories, you went out at night alone?"

"Yes, I wanted to be sure."

"Of what?"

"I'm . . . I'm not certain."

"Did you see anything?"

I gulped. "I . . . thought I did, but I'm not sure. I can't really remember. You see, I felt ill."

"Oh?" The grey eyes were no longer amused. "How ill?"

"Oh, not really ill, I suppose. Just sick, and very giddy."

"I see. And when you got there, you thought you saw me?"

"Yes, it was only a fleeting impression though. Clearly I was wrong."

"You were indeed. What else did you think you saw?"

At first I did not want to answer, but he said sharply:

"Since you have brought me here, Miss Lindfield, at least have the courtesy to reply."

I went scarlet with mortification.

"I'm sorry . . . I shouldn't have. . . ."

"I do not want your apologies. What else did you think you saw?"

I told him what I could remember of that night, and he gave a faint sigh.

"You think I am mad?"

"I think you should go home."

"This is my home."

"Bristol, I mean. This is no place for a girl with nerves like yours."

"I was not always . . . that is . . . I am not nervous."

"No?"

"Well, perhaps I am now, at least a bit. Such strange things seem to happen here, like that woman I saw on the landing."

His eyes narrowed again.

"Woman on the landing? Tell me about her."

I did so reluctantly, and told him what Mrs. Bocking had had to say. He finished his brandy and said curtly:

"If I were you I would get rid of the Bockings. They are doing you no good."

"It's not only them." I could hear the tiredness in my voice. "Other things too, like those toys and the boot."

"Which no one else saw."

"And the letters." I was desperate to make him believe me. "I saw them; I know I did."

"Letters? What letters?"

Drearily I explained, knowing that he was not going to believe me, and avoiding the details of the two notes, for I could not possibly talk of love in such terms to Dion Mallory.

When I had finished, he said quietly :

"I still think you should leave here, unless of course, there is some reason why you cannot do so."

There was a note in his voice which even in the depths of my unhappiness I could not miss.

"Cannot do so?"

"Precisely."

He did not elaborate, and I had no idea what he meant. To cover the resulting gap in the uncomfortable conversation, I said the first thing which came into my head.

"Do you think there are still smugglers here, Mr. Mallory?"

I had expected him to reject the suggestion out of hand, but he didn't. His eyes were travelling slowly over me, as if he were dissecting me with a knife.

"I have no idea," he said finally, and his words were frosty. "And surely the less you were to say about that subject the better."

A warning? I wasn't certain, but I dared not ask him anything else about smugglers or the horses which I had seen not long ago. Instead, I turned to the question of the Cobbs, and young Matilda's unexpected remark.

With the matter of contraband out of the way, Dion Mallory was at ease again, although somewhat acid.

"Why shouldn't two of the brats be visiting their aunt? Must you make a mystery out of everything?"

"But Matilda. . . ."

". . . is a child. Her mother was probably right : she wanted attention. God knows she and the others get little enough of it." He rose from the chair and looked down at me. "I have to go, Miss Lindfield, but perhaps you should go to Rye and consult a doctor. He might be able to do more for you than I can."

It was like a slap in the face, but I got out of my chair without letting him see it. He had another appointment. It was not difficult for me to guess with whom, and that thought was far more hurtful than his suggestion that I was an hysterical female requiring medical attention.

"Of course."

I went into the hall to shew him out myself. There were more lights now, particularly on the upper landing, for I had had enough of spectres. I glanced up at the portrait of my father, seeing that Mallory was also looking at it.

"That was my father."

"I know."

Again he gave me a glance which I could not quite interpret : it seemed half-speculative, half-inimical.

"I knew Julian Lindfield quite well."

I was astonished and said so.

"You knew him? But how extraordinary."

"Not in the least. I often met him in London, and he was a fairly regular visitor to Barley Farm; an old and valued friend of Martineau's." Again the hint of scorn. "Why else should Silas leave you all his money?"

"And you saw my father here?"

"More often in London. I was told that he died in an accident."

I bent my head so that Mallory should not see my sadness, which was a very private thing.

"Yes, he did. A coach overturned, and his neck was broken."

"Most unfortunate."

He was not quite smiling, yet his reaction was far from sympathetic, and my gust of anger made it possible for me to bid him good-night with my chin held high. However rude Dion Mallory decided to be, and for whatever reason, I would not let him know that my dislike of him was now tinged with another feeling which I refused to analyse.

I closed the front door and let him go on his way to Tana, hating him quietly, and Tana even more.

When I next went back to Laura Martineau's nursery, I found that someone had cleared it. All the broken and unwanted furniture had been neatly stacked in one corner, the toys arranged in another. I supposed that Comfort must finally have found time to squeeze the cleaning of the room into the staff's busy schedule, and later that day I thanked her for making a start on it.

"The nursery?" she shot me a look. "We haven't done that yet."

"But it's been tidied up. Everything has been moved."

"Not by me." Comfort frowned. "I'll ask the others, but I gave no orders."

Later still, she said :

"The nursery, Miss Charis. You remember you asked me about that this afternoon?"

"Yes?" I was trying to complete Alicia Martineau's antimacassar, with rather less skill than she had possessed. "Did Emily do it?"

"No, no one did. Are you sure stuff had been moved?"

A week ago I might have given Comfort my emphatic assurance that I was certain, but by now I had learned my lesson. Even Comfort would begin to doubt my sanity if any more of my pronouncements proved foundationless.

"No, not absolutely." I threaded my needle carefully. "Perhaps I just thought it looked neater than before. It's not important."

"I'll get it done to-morrow."

"No hurry." I was very calm and collected. "I should leave it. After all, the room is not used, and there is so much else to do."

I waited until she had gone and then put my work aside. Part of me wanted to wait until morning to check the nursery again, but another part could not resist the temptation to make an immediate inspection. I knew I should never get to sleep unless I had had another look.

The lamp made shadows on the wall as I went on tip-toe through the old part of the house and up the stairs to the attic. They didn't bother me this time, for I knew it was my own light which was creating the wavering blobs on the wall.

When I opened the door of the nursery and walked in my heart sank. Thank God I had not persisted in my questions to Comfort, for the room was a jumble again, the bits and pieces all over the floor, just as I had first seen them.

I stood very still. Was Dion Mallory right after all? Did I need a doctor. Then I ground my teeth. No, indeed I did not. I might have had an upset stomach on the night I went to the church, but I was not going out of my mind, and no one should say that I was. This morning, the nursery had been cleared:

now it was as it was before. There had to be an explanation, and the most obvious one was that someone thought there was still something there which I might find. Something like the letters, which had to be removed before my prying eyes could discover it. It was a sensible solution, until I stopped to ask myself who had been responsible: then I twitched with alarm again.

I began to search, very quietly so that no one downstairs should hear me. After what seemed an eternity I had to admit that there was nothing. If there had been something else, it had gone now. There was one last place to look; a small cupboard on the wall by the fireplace. I opened it and looked inside. It was very dusty and seemed at first to contain only a few books, but then the glint of metal caught my eye and I reached in to pull the object out.

It was a mirror, steel-framed and grimed across its face. I rubbed it with my sleeve, propping the lamp up on a rickety table just below the cupboard.

I could see the whiteness of my face in the semi-gloom, eyes wide and scared, the blood gone from my lips. I was about to put it back when a mist began to cover the glass, and I gave a small whimper, still clutching the mirror which seemed to be sticking to my hand.

I wanted to throw it away from me and to rush away from that dark, unfriendly place, but I could not move. My heart was pounding in my ears, and I was terrified, but I just stood there, watching the mist curl away again as the surface of the glass went black. I saw a face in it for one whole second, but it wasn't mine, and then I did hurl the mirror from me and fled, the lamp jumping up and down in tune with my agitation.

I could hardly hold my sewing I was trembling so, but Emily

would appear shortly and she must not think anything was amiss. I forced the needle into the linen, keeping my head bent low, hoping the fire would soon bring some life back into my cheeks again.

All my self-assurance had gone, exploding into tiny fragments in my headlong flight downstairs. Perhaps I was letting Barley Farm affect me, giving me delusions which wore the outer garments of sanity one moment, and the inner garb of madness the next. No one could have moved the furniture up there; if they had, Comfort would have known. If Emily or Agnes had been set such a task, their complaints would have reached my ears, of that I was sure. And the mirror. I didn't want to think about the mirror, but I forced myself to do so rationally and without panic.

That was more easily explained. I had found a dusty looking-glass which I had held up in the shifting half-light. I had seen my own face, probably clouding the mirror with the warmth of my breath. When I had looked again, I had thought I had seen a stranger, but it must have been my own reflection once more, wilder and more frightened, and the scary atmosphere of the room had done the rest.

Ten minutes later I was myself again. I really would have to pull myself together, or accept Dion Mallory's advice and go back to Bristol. I had a momentary vision of my father's smile, caught for ever on the canvas at the top of the stairs.

"Damn it," I said aloud, not caring how shocking my language was. "I will not be driven away. This is my home, and I am going to stay here."

SEVEN

When Emily came to announce the arrival of Bel Rolfe the next afternoon, I was delighted. I needed someone friendly to talk to, and when she shewed him in, I took his hand and led him to the fire.

"Oh, I am so glad to see you." I let him settle himself in the chair, for I knew he would not like too much assistance. "Emily, some tea, please."

Emily gave Bel a dark look, but she sketched a curtsey and left us, and I took my own place by the hearthrug.

"I was feeling low," I said. "You must have guessed it."

"In a way I did." He smiled, turning his head in the direction of my voice. "But I had heard whispers that you were unhappy. Nothing can be kept quiet in such a place as this, as I told you."

"Whispers?" I tensed. "From whom?"

"I'm not really sure."

He didn't see my doubt, of course, and his low-pitched laugh was gentle, washing away the distrust in me.

"How does one hear rumours?" He shrugged. "They blow about in the wind, especially in Haydore. What is wrong?"

"I'm not sure."

"I expect it's your new surroundings. It is so different here from a town, that you must find the changes startling."

"Yes, probably you are right."

113

"But you're not sure?"

I tried to echo his laugh, but it sounded shrill and unsteady.

"Not absolutely."

"Then tell me about it, and you'll feel better."

"It all sounds so absurd."

"I shan't think so."

It wasn't hard after the first sentence or two, because Bel exuded a sympathy which seemed to fill the room. There was something about him which restored confidence and made one feel warm inside, and even in the middle of my story, I was aware that I was growing very fond of him.

I broke off in the course of my description of the woman on the landing because Emily had brought in a large tray piled with cups, plates, and delicious sandwiches and cakes.

"How are you, Emily?"

Bel seemed to know just where she was standing, and yet again I marvelled at the way he had overcome his sightlessness.

"Well, sir."

She was grudging, but Bel was undeterred.

"And your mother?"

"The same."

"Tell her I asked after her. Has she made some of those scones, Emily?"

To my surprise, Emily's dour face cracked in a smile.

"Yes, sir, just like you used to have them."

"Good. No one makes scones like your mother."

I waited until Emily had disappeared again, pouring the tea and guiding Bel's hand to the cup.

"You have tasted our scones before, then?"

"Oh yes, many times. I used to visit the Bockings when I was young, and always about tea-time." He chuckled and his fingers explored the plate I had given him. "I was a cunning boy, you know."

Suddenly I felt better. Bel was so normal, and he was tucking into a hot scone, oozing with fresh farm butter, as if it were the most important thing in the world.

"Go on," he said at last, wiping his mouth with a napkin. "You were telling me about the woman on the landing."

"Who wasn't there," I said ruefully. "The Bockings said it was the ghost of Mrs. Copper, but since that isn't possible, I must have dreamt the whole thing."

"Easy enough to do when it is dark." Sensitive as ever, he could feel my momentary indecision. "At least, I imagine it would be. For myself, of course, it is always dark."

I said nothing, and he put his head on one side.

"Don't look as I am sure you are looking, Charis. There is no need to be sorry for me, for I am not sorry for myself, and you mustn't be uncomfortable when I say things like that. We are friends, aren't we? There should only be happiness between friends."

"Yes, of course." I said it thankfully, and passed the scones to him again. "I am being too silly about all this. You are quite right, of course, it is the change from such a stiff and starchy place as Bristol, or rather, my aunt's house there. I haven't got used to Haydore yet, and after all, most of the things I've talked about could have quite ordinary explanations."

"Your illness on the night you went to the church? Yes, that's easy enough to understand. The horses? Well." He raised his shoulders. "Even now, people don't ask too many questions about such things, but there was nothing unearthly about the beasts, I'm quite sure."

"And old houses make noises, don't they?"

"Invariably." He was teasing again, but in a very kindly way. "Even my modest dwelling can produce a phantom or two after lights are out. It's a good thing poor old Jonet is deaf, or she'd be as scared as you are."

Somehow I doubted that. Old Jonet did not look the kind of woman to be scared of anything, but I knew he was only trying to stop my worries.

"And the letters you found? Did you read them?"

I hoped my voice would not betray me, for somehow, even to Bel, I could not admit that I had done so.

"Oh no. I just put them somewhere and cannot find them now. I wouldn't read other people's letters."

"I'm sure you wouldn't." He was soothing. "I hear Dion Mallory has called on you."

"Yes." I did not tell Bel that I had asked Dion to do so, and hoped that he would not find out. "He came, and was as rude as ever."

"Poor Mr. Mallory; what a thing it is to be crossed in love."

"But he seems to have found some consolation here." I was waspish. "I doubt that he is in need of your pity."

"Oh?" Bel was very casual, crumbling a piece of Savoy cake with his fingers. "What consolation could he find here?"

"I think he sees that girl Tana." All at once I wished I had not said that, but it was too late now. I could see the change in Bel's expression, hurrying on, trying to repair the damage. "But I might be mistaken about that too."

"I should think you are. He is used to a different kind of woman from Tana."

"She's very lovely."

"So I believe, but I doubt that she would satisfy Mallory. She's a simple girl."

I wanted to tell Bel I thought him wrong, but something

warned me not to.

"You know her well, of course."

"Naturally. She comes to see me now and then."

I gaped, but fortunately Bel could not see that.

"Why not?" He was gently ironic, understanding my brief silence. "We've known one another all our lives, and I told you I had need of company sometimes. She sits with me for a while now and then.

"She lives on apples and roots," I said, and felt stupid as soon as I had said it. "She has a knife on the wall of her shack too, did you know that?"

"No." He finished his cake and leaned back, holding one slim hand towards the fire. "But then, of course, I have never seen the inside of her home."

"Oh Bel, I'm sorry. I forgot."

"Don't be sorry. You pay me the greatest possible compliment when you forget that I am blind. As to Tana's knife, there is probably some quite dull and ordinary reason for it. Perhaps she likes her roots peeled."

"Of course! What else? How senseless of me to make such a to-do about it. Just like I did about that boy, or rather the boy I thought lived here."

"Don't worry about it."

"Do you know the reason for Miss Prentiss leaving so suddenly?"

"Dora Prentiss?" He considered the question for a moment. "No, I don't think I do. I really didn't know her very well. She was a quiet sort of woman, who had a great love of privacy, and we respected it. Probably she had a call from a sick relation, or something like that."

He stretched in contentment and then stood up.

"I could stay here all day talking to you, Charis, but I must go, or Jonet will think I am lost and come looking for me. Thank you for tea."

"You've been so kind, Bel." Somehow we had slipped into the use of Christian names without noticing it: formality and Bel Rolfe did not go together. "You will come again?"

"Of course, and you must come and see me. Jonet shall make you her special honey cake, which is fit for the gods. No, don't bother to disturb yourself or Emily. I can find my own way out."

I did not protest, for I understood why he needed to be self-sufficient, admiring the way he moved slowly but safely to the door. Once there, he turned.

"Good-bye, until next time."

"Good-bye." I gave him a special smile, although I knew he couldn't see it. "You have helped me so much. I might have run away like Miss Prentiss, but for you. Now, nothing will drive me away."

He nodded, and I watched the door close behind him. Dear Bel. He was as handsome as he was compassionate, and no wonder my affection for him was deepening. Then I gave a sigh. Affection, yes, but why could I not nurse for him some of the tormenting thoughts I was harbouring for the indifferent Dion Mallory?

"Because you are a blockhead, Charis Lindfield," I said to myself in some irritation, and rang for Emily to remove the tray.

At eight o'clock I was having dinner. My resolutions about plain food had gone by the board, for never before had I had the money to indulge in good living. I feared I might be getting greedy, for I sat down to Spring Soup, Poulet à la Marengo, and almond pudding, as if I had never eaten anything in my life.

I was just finishing the last mouthful of my sweet when I heard the church bell begin to toll. It was the same soft, mournful note, but this time I listened without fear. If I was going to live up to my promise to myself, I should have to accept the oddities of Haydore, and the ringing of the bell to keep Old Nick at bay was one of its foibles.

I even ignored the creaking on the stairs as I went to bed. True, I paused for a moment trying to locate where the sound was coming from, but I would not let myself be fearful. It seemed to be in the wall between the old and new parts of the house, as if the two halves were trying to pull apart. I dismissed the matter with a shrug. It must be rats; what else could it be?

I was not sleepy, and so I sat by the mirrored dressing-table and thought about Tana, Mallory and Bel Rolfe. Tana always called me pretty Charis, and I found myself hoping that Dion agreed with her. I unpinned my hair, letting it fall about my shoulders, and considered my face critically.

It is difficult to be impartial about one's own reflection. The bones of the cheek and jaw looked good enough, and there was a new redness about the lips which had not been there in Aunt Lavender's day. Even she had said my eyes were large, and perhaps not everyone thought hazel so objectionable a colour. After a minute or two of self-examination I sighed despondently. Perhaps I was pretty, but not ravishing like Tana. Bel had not seemed to like the thought that Mallory might be paying attention to Tana, but that was probably because he had known her for so long, and did not want her to be hurt by someone like Dion.

I had been surprised when Bel said that Tana visited him, although there was no earthly reason why she should not do so. They were old friends, as he had said. What a pity Bel would never be able to see the exquisite face with the dark, slanting eyes, and skin as white and pure as milk.

When I awoke the next morning, it was to a cry from Emily Bocking. She had already pulled aside the curtains to let in a wintry daylight, and was standing by the bedside, my cup of tea rattling in her hand.

"Emily?" I struggled up, still caught in the strands of sleep. "What is it?"

She was staring at my bedside table, eyes dilated, mouth slack with fear.

I turned my head to see what she was looking at, noticing at first only the small enamelled clock, a book, and the Dresden shepherdess of which I was very fond.

Then I saw it, and gave an exclamation of disgust. It was dun-coloured, made of clay, and shaped like a heart. Through it was the pin of my garnet brooch, stabbing into it like a sword.

"Emily! What is that?"

Somehow she managed to put the cup down without dropping it, her face as bleached as my sheets.

"It's one of . . . one of those, Miss."

"One of those what?"

I reached out to pick it up, although the very thought of touching it made my stomach heave, but Emily cried out again.

"No, no, don't, don't! I'll get Miss Risby."

I sat and watched the thing, whilst Emily ran off to get Comfort. I could not even pick up my cup, too shocked to move until Comfort and Emily returned with Mrs. Bocking. All three of them considered the heart in silence. Then Ellen said:

"A warning, Miss, that's what it is. A warning."

"Of what?"

"Not to meddle in things."

"I am not meddling in anything, Mrs. Bocking," I said as haughtily as my shaking voice would let me. "I have no idea what you mean."

"Everyone knows you've been asking questions." Her eyes were so light they were almost like water as they turned on me. "Some don't like that."

"Do you know who put this here?" I demanded curtly. "Was it you, or Emily?"

"Not me." Mrs. Bocking denied it at once. "I wouldn't touch one of them things to save me life."

"Nor me." Emily was equally firm. "Terrible, that's what they are."

"Could it have been Agnes?"

"Not her either." Mrs. Bocking was grim. "She's knows better than that."

"Then what about Louisa?"

The Bockings exchanged a quick look.

"Might have been her," agreed Emily finally. "She's a rum one. Got the eye, you see. Yes, it might have been her. Better ask her, Miss."

And so I did later, but poor Louisa's face crumpled into tears at my query, and it took nearly ten minutes to console her. When I had convinced her that I believed in her innocence, and her tears were dry again, I said slowly:

"But you know what it is, don't you, Louisa? You've seen something like that before?"

She nodded miserably. "Yes, Miss. I knew a woman what got two of those left on 'er doorstep. Not both at once, you understand, but one after the other."

"Like . . . like this thing?"

"One were like that. The other was a . . . poppet."

I drew a deep breath. I did not want to ask the next question, but it had to be done.

"What happened to her? The woman who received these things?"

"She died." Louisa's good eye was scared, the other hiding away in its corner. "Got took bad, and nothin' could save 'er. Everyone knew what it was, of course."

"Thank you, Louisa, that is all."

She didn't scuttle away as I expected her to. Instead she stood very still, her lips moving slightly as if she were trying to say something else.

"Yes, what is it? Something more about that woman?"

She shook her head, as she tried to get the words out.

"No, Miss, not that. Something else."

"Yes?" I could see she was very frightened, and tried to reassure her. "What else, Louisa?"

"It's about. . . ."

She stopped abruptly, face wax-white, turning her head quickly as if she had heard something.

"Louisa! What is it?"

"It's nothing, Miss, nothing."

"But. . . ."

"Nothing at all."

She fled, leaving me staring after her. I could not imagine what she wanted to tell me, nor had I heard anything which would have caused her to take fright. I shook my head in perplexity. I would have to talk to her again another time, when she was calmer.

"How could it possibly have got there, Comfort?" I asked later on when the two of us were alone. "The Bockings were obviously terrified of it, and so was Louisa. Agnes wouldn't have touched such a thing, so Mrs. Bocking says, and I certainly didn't put it there myself."

"Neither did I." Comfort pulled her shawl tighter about her as if she was craving for warmth. "As to where it came from, Miss Charis, I doubt that we shall ever find out. It seems no one does find out about these things."

I was more irritated than frightened by now, the first shock having passed. The thought of someone creeping into my room and leaving such a monstrous insult on my bedside table angered me, and I had somehow managed to ignore the fact that there was no one who could have done it.

"I shall forget it," I said firmly, "and you must do the same. Have you burnt it?"

"Yes, straight away."

"I shall never feel quite the same about my lovely brooch." I was sad about that, for it was my pride and joy. "But I shan't be a goose about it. I'll wear it this very evening."

"Won't you think again about leaving, Miss Charis?" Comfort was busy with the clean underwear she was putting into the chest of drawers. "There isn't much here for us, is there? You've not been yourself since you came, and. . . ."

"We are staying." I was adamant, not listening to her distress. "Let the rats scratch, the bell ring, toys and letters vanish from under my very nose. Even things like that . . . that heart will not change my mind. We are staying, Comfort. I will not run away. What would my father think of me if I did?"

It seemed that I was not destined to keep my shaky determination intact for very long.

Two days after the appearance of the clay heart I jerked awake, feeling as though something dreadful had happened. And so it had, although at first all I was conscious of was the

123

sound of screaming.

I almost fell out of bed, thrusting my arms into my peignoir as I made for the door. It must have been very early, for it was hardly light, and the lamps on the landing table were still glowing. The cries came from the upper part of the house, and as I ran up the stairs I could hear voices and whimperings and then sudden sobs.

I rounded the corner and finally reached the top landing. I could see one of the doors open, and it was from that attic bedroom that the noise was coming. As I went in, I was aware of Comfort, her hand over her mouth; Mrs. Bocking, stiff as a block of wood; Emily, transfixed as she stared upwards, and Agnes Stoop gulping down air as she cried until her cheeks were a blotchy crimson.

Finally I looked up too, and caught at the handle of the door to support myself. There, from one of the beams running across the ceiling, Louisa Cockie was swinging gently to and fro, her body turning very slightly from side to side. My mouth opened silently, taking in the knotted strip of sheet which was round her neck and looped over the beam. Not far off was a chair, knocked over on its side.

"Oh God!"

I managed to say something at last, and the others all turned to me, starting out of their skins as if I were another apparition.

"Miss Charis!" Comfort let her hand fall to her side, her voice breaking. "Oh, Miss Charis, look what that poor mite's done to herself."

"Why is she moving?"

I must have sounded half-witted, but it was all that I could think of to say, and there was something rather awful about the movement of that very dead body.

124

"I touched her." Comfort blew her nose quickly. "I just thought she might be alive, but she wasn't."

"I see." I tried to pull myself together and take charge of the situation. "But what is she doing here? This wasn't her room, was it?"

"No, this one was empty. That's why she came here, I expect."

"But why?" I was bitter at the waste of it all, the thought that my recent questioning of Louisa might have been part of the cause of her action like a lead weight in my heart. "Why would she do this?"

Ellen Bocking shook her head. "Who knows, Miss? She were a funny one, like I said before. Perhaps she'd got herself into trouble with some boy."

I rejected the suggestion out of hand. Louisa's immature and under-nourished body would not have attracted the most easily satisfied of men.

"That's impossible. We should have been aware of it, surely, and who could she have known?"

"One of the village lads, perhaps. Maybe it was something else though."

"I'm sure it was." For a second I remembered that Louisa had been trying to tell me something not two days before. Had she been trying to confess that she was responsible for that clay heart, and, finding she could not bring herself to admit it, taken her life in contrition? "Comfort, go and fetch one of the men. Get him to go to Elmbrook and fetch the doctor."

She obeyed with alacrity, glad to get out of the attic, the others following her without delay. I gave Louisa one last look. She was still now; hanging there limply like a stuffed doll. I wanted to cry for her, but I couldn't. All I could feel was an

125

empty hollowness inside.

The doctor came, and with him a constable from Rye, who happened to be visiting Elmbrook. They cut poor Louisa down, and Dr. Stevenson examined her briefly and without much interest. As far as he and the constable were concerned there was no cause for suspicion. Louisa had killed herself, although neither man seemed particularly surprised. Perhaps they had seen too many Louisas of this world, taking a not very easy way out of a life they found intolerable.

Louisa's body was taken back to Lydd from whence she had come, and that was the end of it, but I couldn't get the tragedy out of my mind.

"If she was so unhappy, why didn't she tell us, Comfort?"

"Perhaps she couldn't. Girls like that find it hard to talk sometimes. She may not have wanted to tell us about whatever it was."

"Dr. Stevenson confirmed that she was not pregnant."

"No, but there are other things folk don't like to speak about."

I had not mentioned to Comfort Louisa's effort to tell me something, nor had I breathed a word of my own doubt that she might be responsible for the heart. Since there was no proof, and Louisa was now dead, it would have been utterly wrong to point such a finger.

"Do you think the Bockings and Agnes upset her with their talk of her evil-eye, hinting that she might be a . . . a. . . ."

"A witch?" Comfort grunted. "Don't suppose it helped none, but they didn't say much to her while I was there."

"She couldn't have been a witch, even if there were such things." I forced my lips into some kind of smile. "If she had been, she would have survived, and one of us would have died."

"Put all that out of your mind, Miss Charis," said Comfort

126

shortly. "Louisa wasn't a witch, but she didn't want to go on, and that's the end of it. She took her own life, and now you must forget it."

"We'll need more help now."

"Maybe." Comfort was on safe ground now, and her colour was returning to normal. "But not living-in. I'll see if one of the Cobb girls can come in for an hour or two a day. That'll do for the time being. Louisa didn't do that much, when all is said and done."

Then I did begin to weep, for it was such a sad epitaph. Poor, ugly, under-sized Louisa Cockie, not out of her teens, had not done much. I felt the tears run down my face, not bothering to check them.

She had done one positive thing, though, whatever Comfort might say. She had knotted a piece of sheet, put it round her skinny throat, and then kicked the chair away from under her. There could not have been a more definite indictment of her world than that.

I went to see Bel and, of course, he comforted me.

"Poor Charis," he said softly, and let his hand rest on mine. "Don't fret, my dear, she's at peace now."

"But I was her employer." I clutched at him like a drowning man at a straw. "Bel, I ought to have seen that something was wrong with her."

"You cannot possibly blame yourself. After all, how much did you see of the child?"

"Not much." Again I saw Louisa's face in my mind's eye as I watched her struggle for words which never came. "Perhaps I ought to have seen more."

"Dear Charis, you could not have stopped this. Whatever made her kill herself it had nothing to do with you. You are

127

gentle and kind, and I am sure Louisa knew it."

"Perhaps you're right, yet I feel. . . ."

"What?"

"I don't know. Somehow I feel that her death is all part of what has been going on since I arrived in Haydore."

"Love, what has been going on?" His quiet laugh and the endearment were as healing as his words. "I thought we'd decided that nothing much had happened after all."

"Yes, I suppose we had. But if there were smugglers still here. . . ."

"But there aren't."

"You can't be sure. You said yourself that no one would talk about the horses seen at night."

"Oh, an odd trip or two once in a while, maybe. It's not a serious problem, and nothing to do with Louisa."

I left him, feeling a bit better, that is, until I met Dion Mallory on his way back to Mortdyke.

He stopped, grudgingly I felt, raising his hat as he inclined his head.

"So now you have another problem to worry about, I hear."

I thought his tone positively cruel, and flushed hotly.

"If you mean Louisa, yes I have. But, as Bel says, nothing could have stopped her."

"Bel?" The black eyebrows rose very slightly. "How friendly you have become with Rolfe. And how can he be so sure that she could not have been stopped?"

"He can't be absolutely certain, I suppose." I felt as though I were defending Bel as well as myself. "He simply meant that she was so unhappy she didn't want to live."

"Really?"

He was looking at me as though he thought I had strung Louisa up to the beam with my own hand, and I snapped at

128

him.

"Yes, really, Mr. Mallory. Life is not a happy thing for all of us."

"Yet it is happy enough for you, isn't it? You have Barley Farm, and Silas's money. What more can you ask?"

He bowed and walked off, leaving me stupified by his insolence. I was still shaking with anger when I got home, too upset to do anything but sit and stare out of the window.

Why Dion Mallory should dislike me so much, I had no idea, but dislike me he certainly did. Sometimes his tongue was less rough than at others, but always beneath the surface there was a mixture of contempt and something else, as if he believed me guilty of some crime. I wished I could dismiss his face from my mind, but that had now become almost impossible. I found myself thinking about him, and seeing him, in everything I did.

I tried again to rationalise, and found it no easier than before. I really could not pretend that all of my experiences since I had arrived at Haydore had not happened. Perhaps some of them were just fancies, but surely not every one of them?

I could not rid myself either of the belief that at the root of it was the murder of Mrs. Martineau and the fate of Mrs. Copper. I suppose Comfort's anonymous letter had started that train of thought in my mind, and Alicia's journal, and my dreams of her housekeeper, had heightened the conviction. Yet really there was no evidence to suggest that Mrs. Copper was not guilty; everyone in Haydore was sure she had been.

Once more I found myself thinking of the boy and the letters I had found, yet the letters had disappeared, and no one had ever heard of such a child.

For a moment I was tempted to give in and go back to Bristol, but then I shook the idea off. I had promised myself

129

I would not run away, and I wouldn't. I had Comfort with me, and Bel was a good friend. I would make a renewed effort to put aside all that had happened, and settle down to a normal existence, ignoring the obnoxious Dion Mallory in the process.

My good resolutions lasted until late evening, when I found that questions were still running round my brain like a horde of exasperating mosquitoes. I think it was then that I decided to go and see Tana again, chiefly because her startling honesty and bald, unexpected utterances promised the most likely source of some enlightenment. I would not entertain for a second the possibility that I wanted to see her again because she had become Dion's mistress; that would have been too morbid and undignified to have borne.

I had become almost as secretive as the rest of the inhabitants of Haydore, and waited until Comfort and the others were settled in the kitchen after dinner before I slipped on my cloak and left noiselessly by the side door. I did not really relish the walk to Tana's shack, but nor did I want to advertise my visit by taking Comfort with me.

I was half-way there when I met Henry Jones. He was as startled to see me as I was to see him, and we both stammered a greeting as if we were a pair of felons.

"Are you looking for night birds, Mr. Jones?" I asked finally, feeling compelled to say something in the teeth of his silence. "Are there many about at this hour?"

"Quite a few." He bit the words off, as if he wished the ground would open up and swallow me, his lanthorn throwing bright patches on to his face and untidy mop of hair. "And what of you, Miss Lindfield? It's late for you to be out by yourself."

"Perhaps, but I needed some fresh air. And what harm can come to me here, in Haydore?"

I felt as though I was deliberately invoking disaster, for almost anything could happen, and I knew it. He obviously thought so too, for he frowned.

"Best get home soon," he advised. "Too dark and cold for you out here."

"I shall be careful, I promise you, and I am returning before long."

I thought he was going to say something else, for he half-opened his mouth. Then he snapped it shut and nodded.

"I'd best be off then," he said awkwardly. "If you should see . . . well . . . never mind."

"If I should see what, Mr. Jones?"

But he had gone, and I was left to make the rest of my journey with the unpleasant thought that at any moment I might see something which I would regret.

My own lantern seemed to be burning rather low, and I looked at it anxiously, hoping it would not go out before I got back to Barley Farm. The prospect of a walk in pitch darkness was more than I could stand.

There was a dim light in the window of Tana's shack, and for some reason I did not walk straight up to the door and knock. Instead, I crept closer to the window and peered in.

At first, I could only see the table where Tana's lamp was, and the corner of the bench where I had sat. Then I found that by shifting my position and standing on a small rise in the ground, I could see the corner of the room where the truckle bed was placed.

I caught my breath, feeling as if I had been hit over the heart. I could see Tana lying there, her naked body as perfectly formed as I had known it would be. There was a man with her, his head and shoulders hidden by shadows.

I tore myself away from the window, although I wanted to

131

go on staring in. I did not need to be told who it was who was holding Tana in his arms; the truth of that was like a hammer in my brain.

I stumbled home somehow. I told myself there was no reason to feel such shock, for I had smelt Tana's perfume on Mallory when he had called to see me. Bel had not thought Mallory would be interested in a girl like Tana, but I had always known that he was wrong.

Yet the sight of them making love was a very different thing from the mere thought of an illicit relationship, and I wanted to throw myself into Bel's arms and sob out my unhappiness. But I could never do that. For one thing, I would not admit to anyone, not even myself, that I cared about Dion, and for another Bel would have been horrified to find that I had been spying.

I closed the side door and went into the sitting-room. The fire was warm and welcoming, the new curtains and covers mellow in its light. I was lucky, Mallory was right about that, although he need not have made an accusation of it. I did not have to live in a shack like Tana, surviving on apples and raw vegetables. I counted by blessings with great determination, but it didn't help.

Just at that moment I would rather have changed places with Tana than with anyone else on earth, shack or no shack. I was shaken by the intensity of my feelings, for I had not thought myself capable of them. I heard someone at the door, and picked up a book, opening it at random.

My wild, unexpected passion was quickly smothered as I saw Emily advance across the floor, and I am sure that she noticed nothing unusual in me as I thanked her in the most ordinary tone of voice for my nightcap.

"My chocolate? Thank you, Emily; how nice."

EIGHT

I was somewhat taken aback when Emily Bocking announced that Henry Jones had called to see me. I had had it in mind to talk to him again, but had never thought that he might have the same idea himself.

I asked him to sit down, but stubbornly he refused, looking more surly than ever in the dull winter light as he stood there towering over me.

"Yes, Mr. Jones?"

He did not seem to know where to begin, but since he had sought the interview, I had no intention of helping him. My questions would come later.

Finally he turned red and said abruptly:

"You shouldn't have been out last night. It wasn't safe."

My unpardonable sin of prying through Tana's window made me angrier than I would normally have been.

"Really, Mr. Jones, I cannot feel that my nocturnal wanderings are any of your business. You were out yourself."

"Not the same thing, and you know it." He was blunt, gaining courage from somewhere to go on. "You're taking risks, you know."

"Oh? What kind of risks?"

Suddenly I was very interested in what Mr. Jones had to say, but he must have seen the change of expression on my face, for he drew back into his shell as if I had pricked him with a needle.

"Never mind. It wasn't safe. Why did you come here, Miss Lindfield?"

"Surely that is obvious." I could see a fine line of perspiration on his forehead, and it reminded me of Henry Mutton. Mutton had had that line of perspiration too, and he had been afraid. Now here was another Henry, and, unless I was not mistaken, he was frightened too. "I came because Mr. Martineau left me Barley Farm. It is my home now."

Jones paused, moistening his lips as if working out his next enquiry, but I decided to jump in with one of my own.

"Since we are having this rather odd conversation, Mr. Jones, let me ask you something. Were you at the church on the 2nd February?"

He had been looking at his boots, rather large and still caked with mud. I thought that Emily would have something to say about the mess he was making on the carpet, but at that moment was more interested in his reply.

He looked up quickly.

"At Haydore Church? No, why should I have been?"

"I just wondered."

"No, I wasn't there, but you were, weren't you?"

"How did you know that?" I was curt, for as far as I knew, only Comfort, Bel and Dion Mallory knew of my visit that night, and I could not imagine any of them informing Mr. Jones of the fact. "Who told you?"

"I forget." He glanced away, shuffling his feet. "Someone, I can't recall."

I was glad that I was in my own home and not out in the barren Marshes with him, for frankly I did not believe him. If Comfort, Bel or Mallory had not informed him, then Henry must have been in the church himself to know that I was there too.

"You ought to go back to Bristol."

He blurted it out like a challenge, and I stiffened.

"I find you impertinent, Mr. Jones," I said freezingly. "I have no intention of going back to Bristol."

"You've done enough harm here," he retorted, his bony chin sticking out alarmingly. "Go away, before it's too late."

"You seem to think me culpable of some misdemeanour, or worse." I was as calm as I could be in the circumstances, rising and edging cautiously towards the bell-pull which would bring Emily to the rescue. "What is it exactly that you think I have done?"

He raised his shoulders and looked back at the carpet as if he had said all he intended to say.

"Don't worry about me, Mr. Jones," I said sweetly, and pulled the cord hard. "Just continue to watch your birds, and write your book. Isn't it remarkable that there arc no rooks on the Marshes? Such a common bird, yet it is never found here, is it?"

He met my eyes for a moment; then shook his head.

"No, it isn't, but there are plenty of other species."

When Emily had shewn him out, I went to the bookcase and took down a volume I had been reading not long before. It was about the Marshes and its wildlife, and the birds to be found were listed at length. Amongst them, as I well remembered, was the rook. Whatever Henry Jones was doing in Haydore, he was not studying birds. I put the book back and considered our rather peculiar interview. He had been angry with me for some reason, and seemed to accuse me, but of what I had no idea.

I wondered what he was really doing there, and whether he was in any way responsible for some of the things which

135

had caused me such disquiet. I doubted whether he would seek me out again, for I flattered myself that I had got the better of him this time. Yet I would have to watch out for him. Henry might look a rough and harmless diamond, but he could well be very dangerous.

After Mr. Jones's visit, I had two days of peace. There were no noises at night, no alarms, and even the church bell was silent. On the third day my fragile peace was shattered.

I went into Mrs. Martineau's sanctum with the vague idea of looking at her diary again. I had not read every page of it, and although the bulk of the journal seemed to deal with ordinary, everyday affairs, I thought it worth another inspection.

The fire was welcoming and I went over to it and warmed my fingers, glancing back with pleasure at the room with its dainty furniture and light drapes. It was a change from the heavier décor of the main house, and I thought perhaps I would take to doing my own reading and sewing here.

I left the hearth and went over to the bureau. To get to the desk I had to pass a settee, and as I did so I glanced down, my mouth drying as I began to back away.

There were three cushions on the couch, pale blue satin, with silk tassels. Two of them were propped stiffly against the padded back of the settee, but the third. . . . I watched the cushion writhe, as if it were alive, and I am sure that my eyes must have been starting out of my head. I could feel a trickle running down my spine, unable to look away from the horror. Then at last I managed to get to the door and back into the hall.

I shouted to Comfort and Emily, but there was no reply, and it took me several minutes to locate Comfort, sorting linen on the second floor. As we got downstairs again, Emily and Agnes came running in from one of the outhouses to see what all the commotion was about.

I gasped out my story and they hurried after me into the sanctum.

I pointed to the offending cushion with a shaking finger.

"That's it. That's the one."

All three heads turned to look at it, and then back at me.

The cushion was perfectly still now, neatly settled like its companions, its tassel lying motionless.

I swallowed hard.

"It was moving! I saw it move! Comfort, I did see it."

"This one, Miss?"

It was Emily who moved forward and picked it up, squeezing it between her hands.

"Yes . . . yes, that one."

"Seems all right now." The transparent eyes were on mine, almost pityingly. "Can't see nothing wrong with it."

"Not now, perhaps, but it was moving, I tell you."

"Moving?" Comfort was chewing her lower lip. "How moving, Miss Charis? You mean it was going along, like?"

"No, no." I was impatient, seeing their disbelief and not for the first time. "No, there was something inside it. Something . . . alive."

"Not there now." Emily punched the cushion vigorously with her hand. "See for yourself, Miss."

She held the cushion out to me, but I retreated hastily.

"Please take it out of here, Emily," I said with as much aplomb as I could muster. "I don't understand what happened, but I don't want that thing in here."

Emily's shoulders moved in resignation, and I knew just what she was thinking. I glanced at Agnes's spotty face, seeing

137

the same look. I dared not look in Comfort's direction, for I could not bear at that moment to find that she too was condemning me for such silliness, and so I moved towards the door, just behind Emily and Agnes.

Later, when I thought about it, I could not be sure that I had really heard what Emily whispered to Agnes. Perhaps that was just as unreal as the squirming cushion. Certainly I could not ask either of them if I had been right, for they would not have admitted it anyway. I dared not mention it to Comfort either, for I was beginning to doubt my own senses.

Yet I could have sworn that as Emily went through the door, she muttered in an undertone to Agnes:

"Only her imps. Better not upset them."

The next day, when I had recovered from my daunting experience, I went to see Tana, this time during the daylight hours.

I took a lot of trouble to get ready for the visit, selecting my gown with care, dressing my hair with tortoiseshell combs, and touching my ears with light perfume. Somehow I felt I had to look my best before taking Tana on again, as if I were competing with her for something, although, of course, I was not.

The small ribboned hat was becoming, perched over my brow, and the furs against my cheek gave me confidence. I stared at myself in the long oval glass for quite a while before I picked up my gloves and purse.

It had not occurred to me that Tana might not be in, and I was disconcerted to find no answer to my knock. I felt rather ridiculous, hammering on the wood, dressed as if I was about to attend a fashionable London tea-party, but luckily there was no one there to see me. I thought about returning home, but decided to wait, at least for a while. Perhaps Tana would not be long.

I stood by the shack patiently. From there I could see a whole stretch of the Marshes, broken here and there by clumps of trees. I also noticed in the far distance some more cottages which I had not seen before, and further off still the spire of a church, looking like a finger sticking up into the lowering clouds.

Thirty minutes later Tana appeared. She shewed no surprise at finding me there, her smile impersonal as she opened the door.

"Hallo, pretty Charis, have you come to see me?"

I nodded, too numb to say much, and followed her in, wishing fervently that Tana had had some sort of fire.

"You're cold." She saw my shiver. "How strange, wrapped up so warmly."

I knew that she was laughing at me for looking so totally out of place, and felt rather ashamed of myself. Her own skirt was dark red and shabby with a patch here and there, and the woollen shawl over her shoulders must have been almost as old as she herself.

"Yes, I'm afraid I am. I have been waiting outside."

She nodded and brought two cups and put them on the table.

"I'll soon warm you," she promised, and reached for a jug from a shelf behind her. "Drink that, and you'll be better in no time."

I did so without hesitation, remembering the pleasant beverage she had given me before. The draught was different this time, but equally palatable, and I could feel the inner glow inside me as soon as I had drunk the first few mouthfuls.

"You must be very clever to make such cordials, Tana," I said humbly, for by now all my pride had gone. I might have a lilac gown with embroidered flounces, and a cloak with sabled collar, but I was a pretty useless person compared with the self-sufficient Tana. The shame went deeper than that. I thought about my misery in Bristol and how I had wept at my lot. Tana's existence was far worse than that, yet she was happy, competent and a whole person. "I suppose your mother taught you how to make them."

The red mouth moved slightly.

"No, I learned myself. My mother could not do such things."

"How long ago did she die, your mother, I mean?"

"A long time ago. I've forgotten." She refilled my cup and sat down, resting her elbows on the table, her long slim fingers linked together as she watched me. "Why have you come?"

She was not being rude. She simply wanted to know the reason for my visit. Tana had no time for social niceties.

"Because I thought you might be able to help me."

She said nothing, waiting for me to go on.

"You see, Tana, some quite extraordinary things seem to be happening, and I cannot find out the reason for them. I think perhaps you may know some of the answers."

Once more the movement of the lips, the lowering of the eyelids to conceal the black, fathomless eyes. I tried again.

"There was the cushion, for one thing."

I explained briefly what I had seen, and what I had thought Emily Bocking had said to Agnes. When Tana made no comment, I went on, somewhat desperately.

"There was the figure I saw on the landing; the moaning noises I heard; the figure in the powder-closet; the heart on my bedside table. Then, there was Louisa's death, and, of course, that night in the church."

Once I had started I found I could not stop, telling her everything in such detail that I felt as if I had bared my soul

140

to her. I had not intended to say so much, but perhaps it was the strong cordial which loosened my tongue.

"And so you see," I said finally, feeling exhausted, and wishing the hard bench had had a back to lean against, "I have to know what is going on. I have thought about it very carefully, and I believe you know."

At last she moved, picking up her cup and draining it, rising to light a lamp, for it was now growing dark.

"I, pretty Charis, why should I know?"

"I don't know, but I'm sure that you do. Please tell me; were you at the church on Candlemas night?"

"No."

"Tana!" I wanted to get up and catch her arm, but something held me back. "Please tell me the truth. I have to know."

"It is the truth." The light of the lamp was beneath her face, picking out its perfect contours, making deeper shadows in the hollows of her cheeks. "I was in Elmbrook that night; ask anyone."

"What about the other things? The toys, the letters, the mirror I found in that cupboard? Are you sure you know nothing about them?"

"Quite sure." She paused a moment longer, the glow still on her face, making its beauty almost unearthly. "It is not me who is trying to harm you, pretty Charis, not me."

"Harm me?" I caught my breath. "You think that someone is trying to do that?"

"Oh yes, that's clear enough, but it isn't me. Will you have an apple?"

I shook my head impatiently. I wanted Tana to say more, but she seemed more interested in the fruit she was biting into with small white teeth.

"But who?"

141

"Ah, that's the question, isn't it?"

"I had wondered if. . . ." I broke off, reluctant to mention Dion Mallory's name to Tana. "It did occur to me that. . . ."

"Yes?" She was watchful now. "What occurred to you?"

"The only people who seem to dislike me, and for what reason I cannot think, are Henry Jones and Dion Mallory. Mr. Mallory is always rude when we meet, and Mr. Jones obviously resents my presence in Haydore. He is not like Bel, who is always so kind to me."

I thought I saw something in Tana's eyes which hadn't been there a moment before, but I wasn't certain. It might have been a trick of the light, or perhaps the mention of her lover's name had caused it.

"Do you think it could be either of them, Tana?"

She finished her apple unhurriedly and stretched her arms above her head.

"Maybe, or maybe it's someone much closer to you than they are."

I stared at her.

"Closer to me? I don't understand. There isn't anyone close to me, now that my father is dead."

"There's Comfort Risby."

"Comfort!" I was incredulous. "Comfort wouldn't hurt a hair of my head."

"Are you sure?" Her voice was soft and untroubled. "She's close to you, isn't she? Perhaps she's jealous of you."

"No, no, that's impossible. Comfort and I are friends. She's a good woman. I've known her for over seven years, and she was with my aunt for ten. No, it couldn't be Comfort."

Tana's smile was very gentle.

"With your aunt for ten years, perhaps, but have you asked her where she was before that?"

142

"What do you mean, before that?"

"What I say. Where was she before she went to work for your aunt? Ask her. The answer may surprise you."

It was clear that Tana was not going to say any more, for she stood up, waiting for me to go.

I think that walk back to Barley Farm on a darkening winter's afternoon was the most depressing and alarming I have ever taken.

At first, I refused to consider what Tana had said, dismissing it at once as beyond the realms of possibility. Then, small nagging doubts began to assail me, and I started to remember things.

When I had first considered coming to Haydore, Comfort had said she knew something about the Marshes. Just how much had she known? I had assumed very little, but perhaps I had been wrong. She had known all about Mrs. Copper too, although she said she had merely read about her in the papers.

I was very preoccupied as I plodded back through the mud, not caring that my lovely skirt was becoming damp and sodden round the hem. I had other things to worry me.

Someone close to you, who is jealous of you, Tana had said. Comfort was close, but why should she be jealous? She seemed so fond of me; had been very good to me during those seven long years. But then, of course, I had been no better than she : Aunt Lavender's servant. Now I was mistress of Barley Farm, but Comfort was still a housekeeper.

I paused outside Bel's house, seeing the tempting light behind the curtains, longing to tap on his door and talk to him about my troubles. But I couldn't talk to Bel, or to anyone else, until I had had a word with Comfort. I could not accuse Comfort on the strength of a sly hint from Tana; that would be unthinkable.

I got back finally and changed into a dry frock, pulling out the combs from my hair, and wishing I had ventured to buy some rouge when I saw my own pallor in the mirror. Fast it might have been, but it would have disguised the fact that I was frightened.

I rubbed my cheeks hard, making the blood come back into them, and then went to the sitting-room, waiting for Emily to announce dinner. That night I had no appetite. Mrs. Bocking had prepared delicious Palestine Soup, which I hardly touched, followed by fowl pudding and sweetbreads, which I played with, finishing with ginger cream and trifle, which I did not even pretend to eat.

Comfort brought coffee into the sitting-room herself to find out why I had not done justice to my dinner, clucking as she poured the steaming black liquid into the hand-painted cup.

"Have you taken a chill, Miss Charis?" she demanded, giving me a searching look. "You want to stop these walks of yours. Too cold here at this time of the year."

I nodded absently, trying to summon up courage to question Comfort about her earlier life. It was made more difficult by my affection for her, but I found myself regarding her as if she were a stranger.

Finally I said :

"Comfort, where did you live before you went to work for my aunt?"

The enquiry did not seem to bother her, and for once she was inclined to stay and chat.

"Oh here and there. Now drink this; it'll warm you up. What made you ask?"

I was very guarded.

"I don't know. I was just thinking about Bristol, and how awful it was. Do you ever think about it?"

144

"Now and then." She chuckled. " 'Specially when I'm getting into my warm feather-bed. Never spoilt like that in Bristol, was we? And as for the food! Well, I swear I'm getting so fat I can scarce do up my corsets. A rare change from the old days, that."

"Yes, it was dreadful. Comfort, did you know my father?"

"Mr. Julian?" She shook her head. "No, I didn't. Heard your aunt speak of him times enough though. Real villain she made him out to be, but I never believed her, of course."

"But you didn't know what he looked like?"

"No?" She was puzzled now. "Why?"

"Nothing."

"I suppose you was thinking of him again, is that it?"

"Something like that. He was very handsome."

If Comfort had known my father, and was aware, therefore, that a portrait of him was hanging at the top of the stairs, she was making a good job of concealing the fact.

"Why did you never leave Aunt Lavender?" I sipped my coffee. "You were free to go, even if I were not."

"Not that free." Comfort's voice had a sudden grating note in it. "Jobs aren't that easy to come by, and if I'd given my notice in, I'd have got a poor reference."

"Surely not." I looked up. "Even Aunt Lavender wouldn't have done that."

"Wouldn't she though! She'd not have accused me of dishonesty or anything like that, but she'd have made sure no decent household would have taken me. There would have been nothing left for me but the streets."

"The streets!"

"Oh yes; that's where most women land up who can't get positions." Comfort's mouth was turning down at the corners. "You wouldn't know, of course, seeing you've lived a sheltered

145

life, hard though it was. Yes, it would have been the streets for me right enough. Besides. . . ."

"Yes?"

"Nothing; it's nothing."

We were getting nowhere, and I decided to take the plunge, no matter what the cost might be.

"Comfort." I took another mouthful of coffee to stiffen my resolve. "Did you ever live here on the Marshes?"

The silence which fell was like a pall, and long before she spoke I knew the answer.

"Yes. Yes, I did."

"You didn't tell me. You said that you knew something of the Marshes, but not that you lived here."

Comfort was suddenly withdrawn, her eyes shifting away from mine.

"Didn't think it was important, Miss Charis."

"Where did you live? Was it near here?"

Again no words for some time. Then she said stiffly :

"Aye, not far off."

"How far?"

She glanced at me, her face almost angry.

"Next village but one. Why do you ask?"

"Because I wanted to know." I wouldn't retreat before her chagrin. We had never spoken to one another in this way before, and part of me was in torment at the rift I could see opening up between us. "I think it was odd that you did not mention such a fact when you learned we were coming here."

"I'd put the past behind me. No point in looking back."

It was possible, I suppose, but I was still not satisfied. Tana's remarks had bitten deep.

"Where did you meet Aunt Lavender?"

At first I thought she was going to refuse to reply, but after

146

a pause she said slowly :

"In Hythe. She was visiting a friend of hers at the time, a Mrs. Goss. I was working there."

"Go on."

Comfort shrugged. "Not much else to say, really. I didn't like Mrs. Goss, and one day when I was cleaning your aunt's bedroom, she came to fetch something and we got talking. She was civil enough then, you understand, and I didn't know what she could be like. She asked if I would like to go and work for her in Bristol, and I thought the change would do me good. I said yes. She said I wouldn't lose by it."

I felt the dull stab of fear again.

"Wouldn't lose by it? What did she mean by that?"

Comfort was flushed, whether because of the fire or some other reason I didn't know.

"I'd rather not say."

"I think you must. What did she mean?"

"Well, she said. . . ."

"Yes?" I was holding my breath, waiting for something which I knew would hurt. "What did she say?"

"That she'd leave me everything when she died."

I felt the sick wave pass over me, making me as weak as a kitten, yet I knew I had to conceal my dread.

"But she didn't leave you everything, did she?" I said finally, and put my cup down. "She left it to me instead."

"Yes, Miss, she did."

Comfort gave me one last look and then walked out of the room before I could say another word.

I went to bed early on the pretext of a headache. I told Comfort that I should be settling down to sleep straight away, and not to disturb me again that night. She had merely nodded, as if nothing had happened between us, but I knew that I could not face seeing her again that day.

I blew out the candle, for I didn't want anyone to see its flicker under my door, but I made no attempt to sleep. Instead, I wrapped a rug round my shoulders, hunching up my knees under the bedclothes, considering my position in a new and very unpleasant light.

I could hear the wind howling, and steps overhead at eleven when the others went up to bed, trying not to admit how everything slipped easily into position, given that Tana had been right.

I thought first about the anonymous letter. That had really been the beginning of my fears, for something about the tale of Mrs. Copper had rested uneasily on my mind ever since. But had there really been such a letter? I had never seen it; Comfort had burnt it, or so she had said.

And then there were the things which had happened at Barley Farm. Could all of them be explained away if one worked from the premise that someone living there had had a hand in the occurrences? Noises? Comfort could have contrived those, if she'd a mind for it. She would have had the opportunity to remove the toys and boot and the letters, once I had told her about them. She could have planted the small bottle in the powder-closet, and put the clay heart on my bed-side table, stabbing it through with what she knew was my favourite brooch.

Things added up horribly, and I cringed in the darkness. She could not have been responsible for the ringing of the church bell, but that was an old village custom, yet she could have brought about that moaning noise I had heard, and even the cry of a woman. The cushion? Could she have put some-thing inside a cover; something alive? She would have had

148

plenty of time to slip back and replace whatever it was with an ordinary cushion before I had had time to find her upstairs.

True, she had been forever urging me to leave Haydore, but that might have been simply a clever move to put me off the scent, just as her attitude to the village witch had been.

I thought about Louisa Cockie, and felt the palms of my hands grow moist. Could Comfort have done that? She was strong enough physically, certainly. But why? Had poor Louisa found out what she was doing? Was that what Louisa had been trying to tell me that day?

Were the Bockings afraid of Comfort? I had thought at one time it might have been the other way round, but now I was not so sure. She pretended not to like them very much, but if they were under her thumb, she could dissemble without any difficulty.

It did not explain my lost boy, but by now I had accepted my own explanation that the love-letters were much older than I had thought, and that the toys had belonged to Laura Martineau anyway. The boot? No answer to that, but I already had too many pointers to worry about without the boot or part of an old sailor's suit.

I sat up half the night, mulling over every small detail again and again. Why was Comfort doing it? Was she trying to drive me away, or send me out of my mind? If the latter, why? Or was she trying to kill me, covering the proposed act with a screen of obscure and fearsome happenings. But again, why?

Then I put a hand across my mouth to stop my smothered cry. Of course I knew why. That, at least, was clear enough, and I could not think why I had not seen the truth before.

On my return from London in the previous November, when I had told Comfort all about my talk with Mutton, Silas's Will, and Barley Farm, I had mentioned one other thing

149

RING THE BELL SOFTLY

besides.

I had told her that I had instructed Henry Mutton to draw up my own Will, and later had explained that he had sent it to me by post, that I had signed it, and returned it to him. She knew, too, the contents of that Will, for I had made no secret of it.

If I died, Comfort Risby would inherit everything I possessed.

NINE

The next morning I woke to find a thick mist round Barley Farm. I had snatched an hour or two's sleep, but it had done me no good, and I had already risen and pulled the curtains before Emily came in with the tea.

I drank it slowly, making it last as long as possible, for I dreaded getting up and going downstairs to face Comfort. I felt as though the foundations of my world had suddenly collapsed under me, and that I was floating about like a piece of helpless flotsam.

All my fears of the previous night were crowding in on me again. I had found the answers to my questions, and those answers were worse than anything I had imagined.

I had suspected Dion Mallory and Henry Jones; thought harsh things about the Bockings; wondered about the Cobbs; certain that Tana was hiding something. Not once had I thought of Comfort as the threat. She had been my bulwark against fear; my safe refuge. Now, I realised that I had not really known Comfort Risby at all.

I took a long time over my toilet, fussing with my hair and changing my gown twice, but eventually I had to leave the shelter of my room and make my way to the parlour.

Emily offered me eggs, which I refused, and then some toast which I nibbled, so that she would not think me nervous. I realised that my head was aching, and that I had got a cold, my throat sore as I managed to finish my meal.

It was then that Emily made her startling announcement. She collected the china, piling it neatly on the tray, and said softly :

"Did you know Miss Risby had gone, Miss?"

I felt my heart miss a beat.

"Gone? What do you mean?"

"She's gone." Emily repeated it, watching my reaction. "Weren't in her room first thing, and she's not in the house now."

I sneezed violently, glad to hide my face in my handkerchief. I do not quite know what I had expected, following my talk with Comfort, but I had not contemplated her total disappearance.

"Are you sure?"

"Quite sure. Agnes and me have looked all over. She ain't here."

"Perhaps she has gone out."

"Maybe, but it's an odd time to go out, in this mist and all."

I was forced to agree with Emily, and, on reflection, I suppose it was the obvious move for Comfort to have made. She must have seen that I had guessed the truth, and decided to go before I could take any action.

"Well, if she has gone on an errand, she'll be back soon." I rose, fervently hoping that Comfort would not return. "You didn't hear her leave?"

"Not a sound, Miss. Will that be all?"

"Yes." I sneezed again. "I think I'll go back to bed for a while, Emily. I feel quite poorly. Tell your mother I shan't want much for lunch. Some broth will do."

"Yes, Miss."

She inclined her head, and I went wearily upstairs. With

Comfort no longer there, I felt safer and anxious to close my eyes. My head was pounding, and I could feel myself shake with fever. The mist outside was almost a fog now, hard up against the house, hiding everything from sight. I wondered where Comfort had gone, burying my head in my pillow and at last letting my tears for her run free.

When I woke about two o'clock, the fog was still there, but I felt a little better and went downstairs. When I had finished my broth I said to Emily:

"I think I shall go out for a while."

Her eyes seemed to look through me.

"In this weather, Miss? You'll get lost."

"I'm not going far. Only to Mortdyke."

I had made up my mind to see Mallory as soon as possible to tell him what had happened. It seemed only fair, since I had harboured more than one doubt about him.

"Won't find no one there 'cept the servants." Emily picked up the soup plate and clanked it down on her tray. "Mr. Mallory's away."

I felt a quick pang of disappointment, not entirely free from trepidation.

"Away?"

"Yes, been gone these last two days."

"Oh, I see. Well then, I shall call on Mr. Jones. There is something I want to discuss with him about his book."

I didn't quite know why I was bothering to explain my reasons to Emily, but somehow I was anxious that she should not know my real motive for wanting to talk to Mallory or Henry Jones. Emily did not seem particularly interested, but she killed my proposal dead without delay.

"He's not there neither. Gone off to Lydd or Rye, or some such place. Went the day before yesterday."

153

She left me with a feeling that everyone round me was melting away, leaving me alone in Barley Farm. I considered going to see Bel, but by then my head was throbbing again, my chill making me realise the folly of setting one foot outside the door.

That afternoon was interminable. I sat in the chair by the fire, piling on more and more coal. I tried to read, but the words swam in front of me, and I had no interest in what they had to say. Several times I went to the window and tried to see beyond the clouded panes, but it was no good. It was like being trapped in a box with a tightly fastened lid. I went back to the fire, waiting for tea.

When I heard the church bell, I started violently. It was softer than ever, muffled by the fog, yet there was no mistaking that it was ringing. I thought the unknown ringer must be a hardy creature to be in the ruins of Haydore Church on such a day, going into the hall to make sure that I was not dreaming. I wasn't. The bell was tolling, and now there was a creaking noise by the stairs. I held on to the newel post, trying to get my breath. Comfort might have gone, but she had not taken all the sounds with her.

I could have sworn that I had heard someone cry out, but it was so faint that I really couldn't be sure, and by then I was ready to hear anything. I forced myself to be sensible, and went back to my chair.

After tea there was another hour or two to kill until dinner. I was dreading the night, when I should have to go to bed and try to sleep. I prayed that tomorrow the heavy mist would be gone, and that I would be well enough to go out. I wanted to see Bel; to talk to him and hear his quiet reassurances as he held my hand.

Mrs. Bocking had prepared a full dinner : soup, fish, entrée, and a dessert. I hoped my lack of appetite would not irritate her, but I could scarcely get a mouthful past my constricted throat.

I swallowed a few spoonfuls of crème caramel, and then pushed the plate away. It was no use. I could not eat, and Emily might as well clear the table. When she did not respond to the bell the first time, I was not unduly concerned, thinking she might be out of earshot for the moment. When she failed to appear at my fourth ring, I left the dining-room, hugging my shawl about me as I made for the kitchen.

I stopped in the doorway, a new and unpleasant sensation overcoming me. Emily was not there, but neither was her mother nor Agnes Stoop. I forced myself into the scullery and then into the pantries, but there was no sign of any of them.

It was then that real fear struck me, as physical as any blow. I spun round, making for the other rooms on the ground floor. They were all empty and in darkness. Then I took a candle and went through into the old part of the house. I could hear the creaking again, but I was too concerned by the absence of the Bockings and Agnes to worry about them then. The old wing was dark and utterly silent. I even ventured up to the first floor, although I could not face the nursery above. It was obvious that no one was there, and I hastened back through the passage to the hall.

I controlled myself with an effort. They must be upstairs in their own rooms, although why they should have gone there at such an early hour, with the table not yet cleared, I had no idea. I almost ran upstairs, glancing in my own room in case Emily was turning down the bed. She wasn't, and I hurried up to the next floor. All the doors were standing open, even that of the spare room where Louisa Cockie had hanged herself. There were no lights in any of the rooms, and somehow I could not risk too close an investigation.

I don't remember getting downstairs again, but I knew I had to get out of the house, fog or no fog. I fumbled with the catch of the front door, but the door wouldn't move. I was almost sobbing under my breath as I wrestled with it, but after a minute or two I could not ignore the obvious. The door was locked from the outside.

I ran for the side door, but that was the same. So was the back door which led out from the scullery. I leaned against the wall for a moment, too terrified to move. I could not think what was happening to me. My realisation that Comfort was dangerous had been bad enough, but when she had gone, I had thought myself safe, at least for the time being. Now everyone had gone, and I was locked in Barley Farm alone.

I exchanged the wavering candle for a lamp, and made for the stairs. I would have to look at those upper bedrooms. The Bockings and Agnes could not really have vanished too; they must be up there somewhere. I had to find them, for to remain alone was to court madness.

My legs were aching as I reached the top landing, and I was out of breath. It took every ounce of my remaining courage to venture into the Bockings' room, and then into the one which Agnes occupied. I crept back to the landing, feeling the tears on my cheeks, when I heard a sound from the spare room.

Frozen, I half-turned and watched the door swing slowly inwards. I gave one scream and ran. In my blind frenzy I was sure Louisa's body was still there, although I had seen with my own eyes the limp little corpse being cut down. I was no longer coherent as I stumbled down the steps.

I believed that I had plumbed the last depths of terror, but I was wrong. In the half-light I saw my father moving towards me, and almost dropped the lamp as my knees gave way under me. It was a full minute before I could get up, and at least two before I realised what had happened.

The portrait had swung towards me, and when I managed to slide past it, I could see the opening behind it and the flight of stairs which twisted sharply back on itself and ran down between the old and new parts of the house.

At first, I thought it better not to attempt to see what lay beyond them, but I was not sure what was upstairs in the attic, and whether or not it was following me, and so after a brief pause I decided to go down.

On the first step, I stopped again, shaken by a new and dreadful realisation. Comfort must be behind all this. It must have been she who ordered the Bockings and Agnes out of the house, telling them to lock the doors behind them. She, who had turned the lights out, and she who was now somewhere in Barley Farm, waiting for me.

I began the descent, hearing the familiar creaking sound as my foot touched the worn treads, smelling dampness and decay as I reached the bottom. Far from Barley Farm having no cellars, it appeared to be abundantly supplied with them, for the passage I was in had doors on each side, and I could see another cross-passage at the end. As there were lanterns hanging on the walls, I left my own lamp on the bottom step and opened the door nearest to me. It was a store filled with barrels and kegs, and bales wrapped in sacking. There was no doubt, then, about the smugglers.

I thought I heard a noise and quickly shut myself in the room I was examining. When I looked out again, I was just in time to see a man turning left at the bottom of the passage. It was only a brief glimpse, but it was enough. I couldn't be mistaken about Henry Jones's mop of hair. I hadn't been mistaken about something else either. Mr. Jones had had a pistol in his hand.

I quaked inwardly. Jones must have come down from the attic, seen the portrait had swung open, and realised that I had found the stairway. Now he was following me to make an end of it. I had known he was not writing a book, but I had not thought of him in the light of a murderer.

I went on, turning in the opposite direction to Henry. This corridor was darker than the first, but at one end a door stood open. Slowly I edged along the wall, feeling my heart pumping violently as I saw the two people in the room beyond. Comfort was sitting with her back to me, her head bent. Tana was talking, for I could see her lips moving, and against one flawless cheek she was holding the sharp knife, caressing her skin with the flat of its blade.

I was stunned. I had by now thoroughly accepted that Comfort was not the person I had thought her to be, and that she was to blame for most of what had happened, but it had never occurred to me that she had an accomplice, least of all Tana. Comfort had called Tana a slut, but obviously she hadn't meant it. And Tana had warned me about Comfort, an odd thing to do about a fellow-conspirator, but perhaps she had known time was running out for me and felt it no longer mattered.

They were whispering together like old friends, so there was no mistake. Was Henry their confederate too? Presumably he must have been, or why else would they all be down here?

I slipped away along yet another arm of the maze under Barley Farm. The cellars seemed endless, and must have stretched right under the house and probably beyond. I came to a point where the corridor widened into an oblong area, with yet more doors. I turned the handle of the first, expecting to find brandy kegs. I could not have been more mistaken.

158

It was a bedroom, with graceful rosewood furniture, a four-poster with heavy silk drapes, and a plush pink carpet underfoot. There was even a brazier full of red-hot coals to warm the room. In the bed was a young woman, eyes as round and startled as mine must have been, her mouth already opening to emit a cry.

I was trying to gather my scattered wits together to ask who she was, and what on earth she was doing in an elegant boudoir in my cellar, when I heard footsteps. Before the girl could scream, I closed the door and hastened on into the next passage.

It was a wrong move, for the steps grew nearer, and panic-stricken I looked about me. Unless I could find somewhere to hide, whoever was coming would soon discover me, for he was moving faster than I. It must be Jones, turning back in his search for me.

Then I saw the tiny recess in the wall and the wide stone shelf which led up to it. I have never moved so quickly in my life. I scrambled clumsily on to the shelf, pulling my full skirts after me so that not a scrap should shew, and waited for Henry to pass by.

I was holding my breath, for the slightest sound might attract his attention. But it wasn't Jones who stalked by a second later, but Dion Mallory, a look of intense fury on his face. I crouched in my sanctuary, biting my thumb to stop the whimper in my throat. Mallory too? Were they all in it? Comfort, Tana, Henry, and Mallory, or was it only one of them who wanted my life?

Certainly the smuggling operation had to be run by more than one person, and I only had the word of the villagers, and Henry and Mallory themselves, that those two had recently returned to Haydore. That could easily have been a lie; they

159

might have been there all the time, on and off, and certainly Tana had been. They must have recruited Comfort almost as soon as we arrived, seducing her into their illegal web. I felt horribly sick. Comfort had not needed much persuasion.

I could not stay in my hiding place for ever. Obviously, Mallory had come down the stairway too, and he and Henry would soon meet one another, and, with Tana's and Comfort's help, would begin the search for me in earnest.

I stopped for one last second to think again about the girl in that extraordinary bedroom. Who on earth could she be, and why such a room as that in the middle of contraband stores? Then I understood. Of course; she was probably another of Dion's mistresses. Unwilling to pollute Mortdyke with such a girl, he had made a home for her, and her predecessors, here.

I was stiff as I slid down from my perch, uncertain where to go next. With so many seeking me out, any one of the half-lit passages could conceal my death.

The choice I made was a bad one, and I was careless in that I did not look round the corner before I began to run. I saw the figure at the far end and stopped, unable to muffle my cry. The man turned, and then I felt a sense of blessed relief flood through me.

"Bel!"

I could not see his face from that distance, but I knew he would be smiling at me in that tender, compassionate way of his, and I let my pent-up breath go in a long sigh as he began to move towards me.

"Oh Bel! How did you know that I needed you?"

He came on, and I heard his gentle laugh.

"I knew."

"But how did you get here?"

"Jonet brought me. I don't know why, but I sensed something was wrong with you and that you were in trouble. Perhaps it is because we have grown close, my dear. When we got here, the front door was open. Jonet led me upstairs to the opening on the landing and guided me down here. She is waiting for us."

He gestured vaguely behind him.

"Bel, someone is trying to kill me." Hysteria was rising in me again, despite his solid presence. "These cellars, which I never knew existed, are filled with contraband. There are smugglers, you see. Henry Jones is one of them; he's here somewhere. So is Dion Mallory. Oh, and I've seen Comfort and Tana too. I knew Comfort was involved in some of those things I told you about, but I hadn't thought that she and Tana were. . . . Tana has a knife; the one I saw in her shack."

"Don't be afraid, Charis. I'm here now to help you."

"But how can you help? Jones has a pistol. What can you do against that?"

For once Bel's blindness seemed to matter.

"Whoever wants me dead, will kill you too when they find us together."

"Do not worry, my dear," he repeated, and moved forward again so that he was only a foot or two away from me, and right under one of the flickering lanterns.

I had never known how many kinds of fear there could be until that moment. I thought I had experienced every shade of terror; every subtle variation of its deadly presence.

I could feel the chill of death creeping over me, as if I were slowly turning to stone. First my feet, rooted to the spot like blocks of ice, the petrifying numbness moving upwards until I could no longer feel my body. Even my cheeks were frozen.

"Bel! There is something wrong with your face!"

I made one last, hopeless effort to move, but it was im-

161

possible.

"Bel!" My voice cracked. "Bel, oh my God! Your face, your face! There is something wrong with your face! Oh no . . . no . . . dear God . . . no . . . your face. . . ."

I could hear myself screaming; even hear the echoes rolling down the empty void behind me in diminishing waves.

Then, as Bel's hand reached out to cover mine, I fainted dead away.

I expected to wake up in hell, if I awoke at all. Instead, I roused to find myself in my own sitting-room, lying on a couch pulled close to the fire. Comfort was next to me, and before I had time to shrink back, I saw the look of love in her eyes and knew without any doubt that I had been completely wrong in at least one of my judgments.

"Comfort." I said it in a very small voice, for shame made me want to cry. "Oh, Comfort, I thought . . . that is . . . I believed. . . ."

"I know, love, I know." She patted my shoulder reassuringly. "I saw it in your face; you never could fool me, like I said. But don't you give it another thought, for I shan't. It's all forgotten. You was scared, and no wonder you began to doubt."

"I'm so ashamed."

"No cause to be, no cause at all. Now, put it out of your mind. You're safe now, and here is Mr. Dion and Mr. Henry to take care of you."

I turned my head quickly. Henry was giving me a friendly grin, instead of his usual scowl. He looked different somehow; all the shy insecurity gone. Dion was just the same, save that the slow smile was nothing like any he had given me before.

"I don't understand," I said finally and sat up, Comfort

162

propping the cushions at my back. "I saw you both in the cellars. I thought you were trying to kill me."

"My poor Charis." There was still a faint note of derision in Dion's voice, but there was something else in it as well, and so I no longer cared. "How very alarming that must have been."

"It was."

Then suddenly I remembered Bel, knowing I had lost my colour again.

"What is it?" asked Mallory swiftly. "There's nothing to be afraid of now, you know."

"Bel! His face! There was something wrong with his face!"

"No there wasn't." Dion gestured to Comfort to pour some coffee from the tray by the fire. "That is the whole point. There was nothing wrong with it."

"But there was! I saw it."

"Yes, but what did you see? What was it about him which terrified you so?"

I paused for a moment, still not comprehending. I forced myself to think back to that dreadful moment down in the semi-darkness. I didn't want to, but I knew I had to make myself remember. Then I gave an exclamation.

"It was his eyes! Of course, that's what it was. His eyes! They were looking at me . . . I mean he was really looking at me. He could see. He was no longer blind."

"He never was." Dion took a cup from Comfort and reached for his cigar case. "I think we had better begin to explain what has been happening."

I nodded, still stunned, but remembering suddenly the skill with which Bel had filled a cup, and found his way out of Barley Farm unaided.

"But where is Bel? And Tana? What has happened to

163

them?"

"Tana is in custody, with the Bockings, the Cobbs, and young Agnes. Bel is dead."

I lay back, the strength draining out of me.

"Bel dead? You killed him?"

"No, not I. One of Henry's colleagues did that. We heard your screams, and arrived just in time to stop him from breaking your neck."

I closed my eyes. Bel, who had been so kind, when everybody else had seemed indifferent. Bel, for whom my affection had grown so deep I had almost wondered at one time whether it might turn to something stronger. Bel, who had wanted to break my neck. Then I managed to glance in Henry's direction.

"One of your colleagues, Mr. Jones?"

"Yes." He nodded. "You see, Miss Lindfield, I'm not a bird watcher, as I'm sure you suspected. I'm a Customs Officer from Rye, and my name is not Jones, but Copper."

"Mrs. Copper's son?" I was taken aback. "You mean she was your mother?"

"Yes. I was brought up by an aunt in Rye, whilst my mother was housekeeper here. I received an anonymous letter a month or two back. It said my mother was innocent, but I always knew that." He was looking down into his cup. "That finally decided me to look into the matter of Mrs. Martineau's death, something which I had put off for too long. I fear, however, I made no progress until now. In any event, my superiors wanted a closer watch kept on Haydore. We've been aware for some time that there was a fairly strong nest of smugglers here. We also believed a very large consignment of spirits was due in from France some time early in March. Two days ago, I began to get worried about the situation and went back to Rye to get help."

"I see." I turned to Dion. "And where did you go, Mr. Mallory?" I was still bewildered. "Did you know about this?"

"I suspected something of the sort was going on, although I did not know who Henry was. I went up to London to see Henry Mutton, for there were far more serious matters which concerned me, and I was sure he knew all about them, for he was Silas Martineau's confidant. I was right. Mutton was up to his neck in all that was going on; well-paid to keep his mouth shut. After I had put the fear of God into him, and squeezed every drop of information out of him, I rushed back here. It gave me a bad moment when I found the front door open and saw that staircase. I thought I was too late. Henry had found one of the external entrances to the cellars and had come up through the house to open the door to his men."

"You said more serious things. But what was going on?" I was now totally confused. "Was Bel the smuggler? And who was that girl in the cellar?"

"Perhaps I had better start from the beginning, if you feel able to listen to a very ugly story."

"Please! I must know."

"Very well; it is this. Silas Martineau was a smuggler, like all his ancestors before him, and your father was his partner."

"Oh no!"

"I'm afraid he was. Once when I met him in London, and he had been drinking heavily, he gave his secret away. Indeed, he almost boasted of it. But Silas had other help too, apart from the local men. His son Mark, and his daughter Laura, had both joined in their father's activities from early childhood.

"Mark? So there was a boy. You said he didn't exist. Everyone said so. Why?"

"I said there wasn't because everyone else was insisting upon it, and I wanted to know why too. I was not entirely truthful, I'm afraid. I was only in Haydore about twice in my childhood and youth, and then I spent all my time at Mortdyke. So when I agreed with what others were saying, they assumed I really did not know of Mark's existence. Actually, I hardly knew the Martineaus or Mrs. Copper, and the locals realised that.

"As to why I did not say more to you. . . ." He looked rueful. "You see at first I thought you were involved as your father had been. I could not understand why Silas should leave his house and money to you unless there had been some very close link between you. After all, if Laura could help her father's men, so could you. When you first started to talk of noises and missing things, I thought you were doing so to conceal your real purpose in coming here.

"Later, of course, I realised that I was wrong, but I continued to pretend that I disliked you, a task I found increasingly difficult, holding you at arm's length so that whoever was watching you would not suspect you had an ally."

For a second his face hardened.

"If I had shewn my friendship, it might have precipitated your death, for I knew someone had to be watching. Whilst I was suspecting you, incidentally, Henry was suspecting me, for, as he said, where better to conceal a shipload of brandy than in Mortdyke."

He flicked ash into the fire and leaned forward.

"Briefly, what happened is this. Your father found out that Silas had another and very profitable string to his bow; he was running a baby-farm. The Cobbs looked after that for him. They have no children of their own; those whom you saw there were simply in their care until they could find customers to take them. Chimney-sweeps need small boys; the pretty ones went to beggars, for they are most useful to such rascals. Young Matilda was right. When the children went, they never came back. Some of them died : their lives were insured, you see. Regular payments made to the 'burial man' from whom they would collect money on the death of an infant."

"How horrible. I have heard of such things, of course, but my father could not have known of this."

"I fear he did. At first he objected, but Silas bought him off by making you his sole heir. Silas didn't mind that, because he really didn't like his son or daughter, and they both knew it. He stipulated that you should not know of your inheritance until you were twenty-one, so that you would have some chance of standing up to Mark should the need arise."

"Oh dear God !"

"But when later your father discovered that Mark had introduced yet another side-line, he really could not stomach that."

"What side-line ?"

I waited in trepidation.

"You saw the bedroom downstairs, and the girl." Dion's mouth twisted. "It is not only poor girls who find themselves inconveniently pregnant and anxious to get rid of their babies. Rich girls do too sometimes, and they and their parents are more than willing to pay large sums for a quiet and discreet abortion. What is easier than a supposed visit to relations on the coast, and then a quick trip into the solitary Marshes. It was even more lucrative than baby-farming."

I was almost in tears.

"I can't believe it ! Who ... actually did. . . ."

"Mrs. Cobb. She's a woman of many parts. When Julian refused to accept the situation, they faked an accident, and saw to it that his neck was broken."

167

For a moment I put my hands over my eyes, trying to see my father's face, but I couldn't. There was just a blur, as if he had never existed. Finally, I said wearily :

"But what has all this got to do with Bel and Tana?"

"Everything. Mark and Laura found out that their father had left his possessions to you not long before he died. They both quarrelled with him and went to France. A month after his death they returned to pick up the threads, only now they had adopted different roles. Mark became Bel, and Laura became Tana. They were very patient; prepared to wait ten years to see whether you would come to Haydore. Had you done so, they did not want you to know who they were. But apart from their caution, I think they enjoyed the masquerade. They were very strange creatures."

"But why did the villagers accept them?"

"The villagers and those living round about, always cared more for Mark than his father. Mark, or Bel, call him what you will, had absolute control over all of them, and it was not only through fear. They worshipped him; he had an almost uncanny effect on them."

"Please go on."

"No, now I think I must go back a little, to Mrs. Martineau's murder."

"Mrs. Copper didn't do it, did she?"

"No, Bel and Tana killed their mother, and planted the poison in Mrs. Copper's drawer with other things to point to her guilt. They didn't like her, nor she them."

"Their own mother! How ghastly."

"Yes, it was. They also killed a young man about the same time. He had seen one of the pregnant girls and recognised her. She was a friend of his, and she told him why she was there. He decided to go to the police. He was my cousin, Charles. I too had an anonymous letter saying that his death was not an accident, and that is why I came back to Haydore. Charles's friend grew frightened of what she had told him, and gave him away to Bel."

"But why did Bel and Tana kill their mother? Did she find out about the abortions?" I was remembering Alicia's journal, and the last two heartbroken entries. "Yes, I suppose that was the reason."

"No, it wasn't that. She was already aware of the smuggling: she had learned to accept that. She guessed also about the baby-farming and probably the abortions, but chose to ignore them. No, it was something else she discovered which made her threaten to denounce her children."

"Not more!"

"Yes, and perhaps the hardest thing of all to stomach. You see, Bel and Tana were not only brother and sister. They were also lovers."

My mouth opened slowly, but I could not speak. I was remembering that when I had first seen Tana I thought I had recognised her from somewhere. Now I could see why. She was like her brother, Bel.

"You found their letters, didn't you?" Dion was watching me sombrely. "And I am sure that you read them."

"Yes." At last I managed to get some words out. "Yes, I did, but they were obviously written by children."

"Their incestuous relationship started when they were very young. When Tana saw that Bel was dead, she flung herself across his dead body in agony. After that, she no longer seemed to care what we found out, and talked quite freely. What she omitted, the Bockings and Cobbs filled in. That is why we know so much."

I listened in silence to the rest of it. Tana had not stayed much in her shack, and I had pitied her without reason. She had lived with Bel, or sometimes at Barley Farm, where they moved in for a month or two at a time. The Bockings had kept it in order, until they knew that I was coming. Then they let things slip, so that the house should have some appearance of neglect.

Although Bel had considered the outside chance that I might one day arrive in Haydore, it had not really occurred to him, or Mutton either, that I would elect to live in the house permanently. They had expected me to agree to sell, in which case Bel would have bought Barley Farm, for that would have been the simplest solution, and he was rich enough to afford to do so.

When he learned that I had decided to live there, he and Tana planned to kill me. Mutton had confessed to Dion that upon my death, the house would revert to Bel, a fact which Mutton had deliberately concealed from me. Barley Farm, with its vast cellars and hidden outside entrances, was too valuable for Bel to lose.

When Henry and Dion arrived in Haydore, Bel and Tana knew they would have to be careful, and could not simply murder me out of hand. Henry or Dion might have asked awkward questions. Instead, they hoped to frighten me into a state where my eventual suicide would prove a surprise to no one.

The Bockings and Agnes Stoop had affected a reluctance to work for me, but that had merely been a blind, for Bel had told them to secure the positions in order to carry out his instructions.

Now other things were clear too. Barley Farm not only had ample cellars, it had numerous secret passages, priest-holes and the like. It had been very simple for the Bockings to contrive the mysteries and the fear, and also to watch my every move. There was even a cavity inside the sitting-room fireplace where a person could stand and hear everything which was said in the room, notwithstanding the fact that the fire was alight.

The giant shadow was easily managed, when one knew how; organ pipes in a cupboard with a broken back, so that the wind howled through them, had created the moaning noise; a cushion filled with eels which abounded in the dykes all about Barley Farm, quickly removed when I went in search of Comfort. Agnes had put the clay heart on my bedside table; Ellen Bocking had prepared the small bottle and hidden it by the powder-closet. She had also made my phantom man, by propping old clothes on a stand. The "ghost" of Mrs. Copper had been Emily, using garments which had belonged to the dead woman, and a wig. Once she had seen me run, she had quickly removed them and gone back to the pantry and the pickles. The cry I had heard was one of the girls in the cellar, who had taken fright and reached the top of the staircase.

Tana had spread the rumours of the witch; Isaac Cobb had rung the church bell, not to drive off the Devil, but to give warning that rum and brandy were on their way. Tana had also admitted that an hallucinatory drug had been put in my chocolate on Candlemas night, and that Comfort had been given a sleeping draught to make sure that she did not follow me.

Tana had even boasted of her skill in mixing hemlock and aconite in such proportions that it not only produced a confusion of the mind, made the heart beat faster, the limbs robbed of their natural movement, but also brought about the sensation of flying or rising from the ground.

Tana had been reticent about only one thing: just what had happened in the ruined church that night. Neither she, nor the Bockings would say anything of that occasion, and I would never know whether my experiences were due entirely to that drug, or whether there had been something else there, too terrible to think about.

Bel and Tana had forgotten the toys in the nursery, and also the letters. When Emily heard me mention them to Comfort, they were quickly removed. Since there were plenty of places from which Emily or Agnes could watch my every movement, even the hiding place under my bedroom carpet had been spotted.

"That explains the mirror too, I suppose," I said at last, when Dion had finished speaking. "How was that done?"

"Mirror?" he frowned. "No mirror was mentioned."

I sighed. "Then it was just my own face that I saw, but it was very queer. A mist came over the surface of the glass, and then it went quite black. When I saw the face, I did not think it was mine, but, of course I was wrong."

"Maybe not." Henry's face was serious. "Not everything can be explained, you know."

"Oh?" Mallory was disbelieving.

"No." Henry was not put off by Dion's expression. "Did you know that Bel is short for Beelzebub, and that Tana is the Etruscan name for Diana, the goddess of the witches? I may not have read much about birds, but I have read about Diana and like things. She was the first being created, according to myth: the lightness and darkness of the world. Then she divided herself, and thus her other half became her brother, Lucifer. Diana fell in love with her brother, because of his beauty, and seduced him. There is much more, but, as you see, they were brother and sister, and lovers too."

"Rubbish," said Dion curtly. "The whole thing was a hoax to heighten the atmosphere they were trying to create."

"Apples have always been associated with witches." Henry did not appear to have heard Dion. "Tana loved apples. When she threw herself over Bel's body, I saw that she wore a garter on her leg. The garter is the insignia of rank in a Coven. Another odd thing. The Lovelace daughter who vanished many years ago was not really called Joan at all; her name was Tana too."

"This is ludicrous." Dion was growing really angry. "Henry, you can't possibly believe in such nonsense."

"Perhaps not, but there are magic mirrors, you know. It is said that one can see in them the face of the one who is going to harm you."

"Poppycock!"

"She didn't cry either. Tana was distraught to the point of insanity as she screamed Bel's name, but she didn't shed a single tear. Witches cannot shed tears, you see."

"Enough!" Mallory silenced Henry with a swift and definite motion of his hand. "We have heard enough of this."

Henry reddened, and I said quickly:

"And Louisa? Did Bel and Tana kill her too?"

"She was killed on their orders. Louisa found out about the secret passage, and she had to be silenced. She wasn't one of them, but a stranger from Lydd. They couldn't trust her."

"So that's what she was trying to tell me." I gave Comfort a brief and guilty look. "I thought it was something else. Poor Louisa."

We talked for a while longer, filling up gaps, and then Henry left, Comfort shewing him to the door. Dion was watching me, a faint smile on his lips.

"You can't stay here."

"No, I know. I couldn't bear it, yet I can't go back to Bristol either."

"Poor homeless Charis. It looks as though you'll have to come back to London and live with me, doesn't it? After we are married, of course."

I was confused again, as I tried to hide my happiness.

"You do not have to offer marriage. You have done enough to help me."

"I want to marry you, and don't pretend that you object. I'm not a fool, and I know a great deal about women. I know the exact moment when you stopped disliking me and began to feel something quite different."

"Oh dear, was it that obvious?"

I felt I ought to have been experiencing mortification, but instead I wanted to lean forward and kiss Dion.

"Yes, that obvious, to me at least."

My smile faded for a moment and I looked at him doubtfully.

"I have to tell you something. I thought at one time that you and Tana were . . . were . . . lovers." I stammered over the word a bit, and then made a clean breast of my sins. "I went to her shack one evening and saw her making love to a man. I thought that it was you."

"Undoubtedly Bel, and certainly not me. I found her utterly repulsive."

"Repulsive!" I stared at him in disbelief. "How could you have done so? She was so beautiful."

"To your eyes, perhaps, but you are a woman. I told you that I have had much experience of women, and I knew at once that there was something unnatural about her. She revolted me, although I did not know why. I did go and see her once or twice, because I thought she might know something about what was going on, but I did not touch her. I never could."

174

"Do you think Comfort has forgiven me?"

"I'm sure of it. She loves you."

"What happened to her? I suppose they took her to the cellars."

"Yes, Isaac Cobb and the Bockings did that."

"I saw her. I thought she was talking to Tana."

"Tana may have been talking, but not Comfort. Comfort was drugged."

"Oh dear, how horrible for her." I had a lot to make up to Comfort. "That only leaves the anonymous letters, doesn't it?"

"Yes. Bel and Tana had nothing to do with them, and certainly no one else in Haydore sent them."

"I think it was Miss Prentiss."

"The governess? Yes, very likely. Indeed, almost certainly, for there is no one else. She must have known what was going on, or at least guessed at most of it. Tana mentioned her. She and Bel realised that Dora must have had some doubts about them, but they thought her sufficiently frightened to keep her mouth shut. Even when she ran away, they were confident that she would not speak. It seems that for once they were careless. I suppose the poor wretch could not bring herself to go to the authorities with her suspicions and so she wrote the letters, hoping someone would take notice of them and do something, although how she knew of Comfort Risby I don't know."

"May I see your letter?" I asked. "I never saw Comfort's, for she burnt it."

"Of course." Dion took it out of his pocket and gave it to me, taking the opportunity to bend and kiss my cheek. "Here it is."

My warm blush of pleasure faded as I opened the letter and said shakily:

175

"Oh no! I cannot believe it."

"What is it?" Dion's arm was round me. "Charis, what's wrong?"

"I'm not sure that I know." I was trembling against his shoulder. "Dion, come with me, please."

"Where? My dear girl...."

But I was already picking up a lamp and hastening through to Mrs. Martineau's sanctum, opening the compartment in the desk and taking out her diary. By then, Dion had lit two more oil-lamps, so that the room sprang to life round us.

"Well?" He was almost impatient. "Why are we here?"

I opened the journal, holding it close to the light, Dion's note next to it. Together we stared at them without speaking. Every loop and curl was the same; not a single stroke or punctuation mark was different.

Finally we looked at each other, still silent, even the sceptical Dion unable to find an explanation for what lay before us. How could he find one? There was no explanation, and no mistake either.

The writing in Alicia Martineau's journal, and that of the letter I held in my hand was identical.